GONE
MISSING

A Dusty Burns Adventure

DAVE HAMMER

GONE MISSING: A DUSTY BURNS ADVENTURE
Copyright © 2022 by Dave Hammer

ISBN: 978-1-4866-2254-2
eBook ISBN: 978-1-4866-2255-9

Word Alive Press
119 De Baets Street Winnipeg, MB R2J 3R9
www.wordalivepress.ca

WORD ALIVE
—P R E S S—

Cataloguing in Publication information can be obtained from Library and Archives Canada.

CONTENTS

ACKNOWLEDGMENTS

TO NANCY RUE, FOR ALL your thoughts, insights, and brainstorming sessions on the first draft.

To Larry Warren, who knows his guitars and told me about the 1970 Martin D35.

To Troy Cherniwchan, who instructed me on the ins and outs of forklift driving and helped me pick out the cars that appear in the book.

To all those who cheered me on as I wrote this book. You know who you are.

CHAPTER
ONE

IN A DARK BASEMENT ROOM, a single lightbulb burned, giving off little light. Outside, rain lashed the window. Lightning flashed and thunder shook the house, making the lone lightbulb swing.

A sinister-looking man, Craggy "Crackers" McBean, sat at a square table talking to three others, two men and a woman. One of the men was huge and heavily muscled, whereas the second was short and fat. The woman was slim and petite.

"I have a job for us," Crackers said.

"What kind of job?" asked Peter Grimsby, the fat man.

Crackers stared at him for a moment. "My nephew in Trimble has notified me that the bank is holding money for the Tumbleweed Casino while they conduct repairs on one of their vaults."

"How much money are we talking here?" asked the woman, Vi Scarsby.

Crackers glared at her. The woman's given name was Viola, but the last person who'd called her that had soon come to regret it.

"The scuttlebutt is five million," he said.

"What happened to the casino's vault?" wondered Grimsby, shifting in his seat.

"If you're not interrupting, you're asking dumb questions." Crackers rolled his eyes at the fat man.

The other man's huge forearms rested loosely on the edge of the table. Jackson Tate looked like he could snap a barbell in half. "I'm not going back to jail!"

"There's no chance of that happening," Crackers spoke again, his voice low and as soft as thin bark. "We hit Trimble, then bring the money back and sit on it until the heat cools down—"

"Could you repeat the plan?" Vi crossed her legs. "And tell us again how you know the money is there."

"I figured you'd be the one who would want to know every detail. As I said, the casino has to repair their vault, which could take a couple of weeks according to local gossip. In the meantime they've transferred a very large sum to the vault at the bank. That's where we come in. We go in, snatch the money, and then—"

"Where do you plan to store all that money?" Grimsby leaned back in his chair as if trying to create more distance between them.

"Could you let me finish?" Crackers paused for a moment. "No arguments? Good. Then as I was saying, we'll bring the money back here and sit on it. I've just recently come into possession of a new property, which I put under my ex-wife's name. We'll hide the money there."

"And the money will be perfectly safe?" Grimsby seemed unconvinced. "How will we haul it all over here without raising any suspicion?"

"It's foolproof!" Crackers snarled. "We won't be easily noticed. The chance of anyone seeing us is slim since it's in the warehouse district. Now, we will need fake names... something to call you during the heist." First he turned to Jackson. "You'll be the Hulk." Next he turned to Vi. "And you can be Peter Pan."

"Why do I get a boy's name?" she asked.

"To throw people off the truth."

Vi nodded, apparently satisfied. Jackson smiled, obviously liking his fake name.

Crackers turned at last to Grimsby. "Now, since you interrupted me numerous times and asked idiotic questions, you will be Dopey."

The fat man looked less than thrilled.

"Last but not least, there's me," Crackers continued. "I think you can call me Sherlock."

They all nodded.

"When are we doing this job?" Vi asked.

"In two days," said their leader. "I'll bring everything we need, including most of the stuff we used on the last job. It's a four-hour drive to Trimble, and the bank there, like every typical small town bank, doesn't open until 10:00. So we'll meet here, the day after tomorrow, at 5:45 a.m. Don't be late!"

Suddenly hearing a scurrying sound, Vi peered around the dark basement. "Do you have rats?"

"Possibly," Crackers replied.

She stared at him momentarily, then quickly got up and fled the room. The other two men followed at a more leisurely pace.

When Crackers was alone once again, he smiled to himself. It was a very unpleasant smile.

CHAPTER

TWO

THE TOWN OF TRIMBLE, LOCATED on the South Saskatchewan River, baked in the hot summer sun as Janice stepped outside the bank and shaded her eyes against the glare. There were still a few minutes before the bank opened at 10:00 a.m., but she just needed a breath of fresh air after the boring, stuffy office meeting.

"Two minutes and then you'd better be at your desk," Mr. Clemitt said as he followed her.

Janice turned and saw her boss leaning out the door, tapping his watch. He wasn't a bad boss, as long as she didn't slack off. There was nothing he seemed to hate more than slackers.

She moved aside so she wasn't blocking the entrance and took a deep breath. The breeze still had a tinge of coolness, but it wouldn't last long. There wasn't a cloud in the sky—and if the day before had been any indication, today was going to be a scorcher.

Janice spied an old Bassett hound lying in the shade two doors down. The dog lay on its haunches, its long pink tongue hanging out. She heard the buzz of flies and noticed the dog snap at something. Likely a fly that had ventured too close.

The dog went back to panting.

I hope you won't be out too long, big fella, she thought. *It's only going to get hotter.*

Further down, she noticed a black Buick parked by the curb. As she stared at the car, its doors opened and four people emerged wearing long trench coats and white masks. Either that or they had painted their faces white. She also caught a glimpse of some kind of shotgun or rifle under one of their coats.

Warning bells went off in her head. Panicked, she fled back inside and almost collided with two customers just entering the bank.

What do I do? Should I press the silent alarm? But nothing has actually happened yet.

She looked frantically for Mr. Clemitt. Where was he? She hadn't been outside long.

Then she saw him just outside his office and hurried towards him. "Mr. Clemitt!"

He looked up, his face registering anger. "Why aren't you at your computer? Get—"

"But Mr. Clemitt! They're coming—"

He held up a hand for silence and then, with a very stern look on his face, pointed towards her workstation.

"They have guns!" she added.

Mr. Clemitt's face went as pale as his shirt. He ran to the silent alarm—and hesitated.

"Are you absolutely sure?" he asked.

Suddenly the lights went out—the monitors, even the light on the silent alarm, everything.

Mr. Clemitt reacted quickly, stabbing at the silent alarm button repeatedly with his thumb even though he had to know it wasn't doing anything. He had been too late.

Four people wearing white masks suddenly walked into the bank. They pulled out shotguns.

"Everyone down on the floor. Now!"

Once the four were inside, they posted a sign on the door that read *"Gas leak: temporarily closed."*

Scared, Janice suddenly didn't feel well. She noticed that one of the robbers was tall and skinny and moved like he was older. Another was a huge muscular man and the third was short and plump, waddling like a duck. The fourth was short and slim.

I wonder if that's a woman.

Her thoughts were interrupted by the skinny man's hollering. "This is a bank robbery! Work with us and no one gets hurt. The power is down so none of your alarms work. There's no need to push the silent alarm."

Janice's mouth went dry. Who were the idiots who had fired the security guard, deciding instead to rely on technology? Nothing could help them now with the electricity out and the vault door standing wide open. And it would remain open until the power was restored.

She looked down at her hands and noticed they were shaking.

"I want all four of you tellers to come out from behind your counter!" shouted the leader, who added that they should call him Sherlock. "Bring your cell phones with you. Keep your hands in the air as you come out."

The other three robbers fanned out, their shotguns up and ready to fire at anything.

When no one moved Sherlock yelled, "Now!"

Janice quickly reached her desk, removed her cell from her purse, and followed the three other tellers out from behind the counter with her hands raised, the cell in her right hand.

As she came out into the open, she felt vulnerable and her legs started trembling. She collapsed, her body pitching onto the floor.

A pair of strong hands reached down and helped her up. She looked up and was surprised to see that it was elderly Mr. Peabody, one of the customers. He was much stronger than Janice would have ever thought.

"Don't worry," he said softly so no one else could hear. "It's just nerves."

He steered her over with the others, then stood beside her and put his arm around her waist to support her. He gave her a bit of a squeeze.

Janice felt herself relax a bit.

Mr. Peabody gave her a calm look. "It'll be all right. God has everything in control."

"Who has the keys to the front door?" Sherlock called out. He looked around and spied Mr. Clemitt still standing outside his office. "You there, come here."

When Mr. Clemitt didn't move—he was probably frozen in fear, Janice thought—Sherlock levelled his shotgun at him.

"I'm not going to ask twice!"

Mr. Clemitt snapped out of it as soon as he saw the shotgun pointed at him.

"Of course, whatever you want," he said, hurrying forward. "J–just don't shoot."

"Lock the front door," Sherlock barked.

"Y–yes," the manager stuttered, then fished the keys out of his pocket. He always came across as so tough and in charge, but now Janice saw all that crumble and the real Mr. Clemitt emerge.

Once the door was locked, Mr. Clemitt joined the rest of the staff and customers as they were herded into a corner and told to sit with their backs against the wall and their legs straight out in front of them with their ankles crossed.

Janice followed the instructions as though she were sleepwalking and this was just a bad dream.

"Very good!" said the leader. "Now, hand over your cell phones to the Hulk here."

Once everyone had lined up, Sherlock pointed to the biggest robber.

"Here, Dopey, catch," the Hulk said as he tossed his shotgun to the fellow who walked like a duck. Then the Hulk approached the line of people with a small burlap bag, opening it as he went. "Put all your cell phones in here."

The Hulk went down the line, one by one.

One of the customers looked guilty and his hand shook as he placed his cell phone in the bag.

"Do you have any other phones on you, mister?" the Hulk asked.

The man looked to Janice to be in his early fifties. He had on a blue dress shirt, black dress pants, and dark wingtip dress shoes. His hair was short and greying.

"No, no… none," the man stammered.

The Hulk dropped the bag of cell phones, yanked the man off the floor, and searched him thoroughly. He found a second phone in the man's back pocket.

He spun the customer around and yelled in his face. "I thought you didn't have any more!"

The customer gulped and turned pale.

The Hulk turned to Sherlock. "What should we do with him, boss?"

"I should shoot you for that!" Sherlock said, looking at the offending man. "Collect the rest of the cell phones while I think of what to do."

Janice covered her mouth with her hand. Surely they wouldn't shoot a man just for having a second phone on him.

Having Mr. Peabody right beside her gave her a sense of peace. As she looked down the line of people, she noticed that some looked scared, while others looked resigned. Mr. Peabody, however, just seemed relaxed, as if he were at home entertaining these people.

Janice turned her gaze back to Sherlock just as he started to speak.

"No, I'm not going to shoot you. Not yet anyway," Sherlock said, looking at the offending customer. "Peter Pan here is going to guard you, just to make sure you don't try anything while the rest of us are in the vault."

The remaining robbers hurried into the vault. As they moved, Janice saw that the one called Dopey had a medium-sized duffel bag in one hand. It didn't look empty.

Once they disappeared from sight, Janice couldn't hear much despite straining to do so.

It seemed only a couple of minutes passed before the robbers carried eight bulging duffel bags out of the vault.

The other seven duffels must have been inside the one Dopey carried in, Janice realized.

She knew for a fact that most of the cash in the vault was from a nearby casino and the bills were mostly smaller denominations.

When all the robbers were out of the vault, they hauled Mr. Clemitt to his feet and made him unlock the front door.

Janice watched wide-eyed as each robber put their shotgun into the bags, picked up two at a time, and swung them over their shoulders. The Hulk lifted the bags as though they were empty. Sherlock and Dopey did all right with their bags, but they didn't make it look as easy. Peter Pan staggered a bit under the heavy load.

The Hulk went out first, followed by Dopey and Peter Pan.

At the door, Sherlock turned and stopped. Setting down his bags, he pointed to Mr. Peabody. "You there! You're coming with us."

Mr. Peabody got to his feet quite easily and walked over to Sherlock.

Sherlock pulled his shotgun out of one duffel to cover Mr. Peabody. "Here, make yourself useful and carry one of these bags."

Janice watched transfixed as Mr. Peabody hoisted the strap of the duffel over his shoulder.

Sherlock pointed him to the door with his shotgun. Mr. Peabody opened the door, then turned his head to look at the rest of those in the bank. He winked in Janice's direction and stepped outside.

With his shotgun tucked under his coat, Sherlock caught the door before it closed and followed Mr. Peabody out. With that, the door closed behind them.

CHAPTER
THREE

"FIVE MILLION DOLLARS! THAT'S WHAT I'm talking about," Grimsby hollered as they left Trimble behind.

"Calm down," Crackers said. "Now, don't start spending the money in your heads. We have to sit on it for a while until things calm down a bit."

"For how long?" Grimsby asked.

Crackers turned around in the front seat to glare at the fat man. "For as long as it takes."

Meanwhile, Jackson was driving the Buick while Vi sat in the back seat next to the fat man.

"So what do we do with the money until then?" asked Vi.

"I have a plan," their leader said. "As we've talked about before, I have a place in the warehouse district of Duggan. We'll stash the money there."

Vi frowned. "That's all fine and dandy, but a lot of people work in the warehouse area. How are we going to get the bags of money in there without someone noticing?"

Crackers was silent for a moment, deep in thought. "I've got it," he said, snapping his fingers. "We can host a wedding. I'll put out the word. I'm sure there's someone looking for a place to have their wedding. It's summer, after all."

"Do you figure that will take long, boss?" Jackson's eyes were on the road ahead.

"I'm hoping it can all be arranged in a week. All I need is someone desperate for a venue. I'll let you three know as soon as I have a wedding lined up."

"Even then, how will we get the money into the place?" Vi asked. "I mean, if we're spotted hauling in multiple duffels… it will look odd, even for a wedding…"

"Good point." Crackers scratched his chin. "Okay, we'll get a few service carts, the kind hotels use to deliver food when guests order room service. We can put the money on the shelves and cover the whole thing with a white sheet. It will look to any casual observer like we're bringing in food."

Vi smiled. "That sounds like a stellar plan. Now, I'm beat. We had to get up in the middle of the night for this job. I need a nap."

CHAPTER
FOUR

INSPECTOR JOHN BAXTER OF THE RCMP hurried to his boss's office in Regina. He knocked and, without waiting for a reply, flung the door open and entered. His boss, Superintendent Sanderson, looked up from behind piles of paperwork, looking surprised.

"What's the rush, Baxter?"

"There's been a bank robbery in Trimble. Five million was taken!"

Sanderson sat up straighter. "What? How is that even possible with all the security in this day and age?"

"They cut the power, sir."

"What about their security guard?"

"They let him go after they got a new security system, sir."

"Hmm, that's unfortunate. How many bank robbers were there?"

"Four, sir. Plus they had shotguns."

"Shotguns?" Sanderson said. "Maybe it's good they let their security guard go. He or she might have tried to stop them and gotten injured. Or even worse, killed. What other details do you have? Also, do we know why a small rural bank had five million on hand?"

"From what I've discovered, the local casino had an explosion in their boiler room, damaging one of their vaults. So they moved the money to the bank while they made repairs. And I know what you'll be asking next... the thieves took all the customers' cell phones. With the power cut, there was no way for anyone to contact the police from the bank. However, a man was conscripted to carry one of the bags of money. The bank has informed me that the bills were all small denominations. Mostly tens and twenties. With five million and five duffels, those bags would have been very hefty—easily more than a hundred pounds in total. Some close to two hundred! Anyway, according to the man who helped carry the bags out to the car, the robbers all referred to their leader as Sherlock. After helping load the money into the trunk, the man was left standing alone on the sidewalk with the bag of cell phones beside him. When the robbers were gone, he hurried into the nearest business and called the police."

"That was smart of him to run into a building instead of wasting time rooting through the bag of cell phones to presumably find his own," Sanderson said. "Did he happen to give a description of the vehicle?"

"He did, sir, and we have a bolo out on it now. But I'm thinking it was likely stolen, otherwise they would never have let the man see it and live. Once we find the car, it will hopefully give us a clue as to what direction they took."

"Good job, Baxter. Now, if that's all you have right now, I have to get back to this paperwork. Keep me informed."

"Of course, sir. I'll let you know once I have more information."

With that, Inspector Baxter turned and left the superintendent's office, pulling the door closed behind him.

CHAPTER
FIVE

One month later

DUSTY BURNS SAT ON A hard wooden chair—and he was mad. He'd been hauled in here as if he were a criminal. Pushed and shoved into this room, in a stumbling run, feeling like an idiot.

Okay, so he'd borrowed some money and hadn't paid it back yet. That didn't make him a criminal. He sat in his hard chair, back ramrod straight, and stared belligerently at the loan shark. The Grub. Everyone called him that.

Well, maybe not everyone. Probably not the people who worked for him. But everyone else did. The man's real name was Eddie Grubinski.

The Grub, perched on the edge of his desk, glared back. He let one leg dangle while the other was firmly planted on the floor.

Two very large men stood behind Dusty, each with a large hand on his shoulder to keep him in place. The two men were so close that Dusty could feel their body heat. The air of intimidation was palpable.

Does he think that by sitting on the front of his desk, as if this were a friendly meeting, he's going to make me feel like we're all buddies here? Dusty wondered.

"To say I'm very disappointed in you, Dusty, would be the understatement of the year," the Grub spoke in a conversational tone. "I took a chance on you, even though you're very young. Obviously I was wrong! Did you think no one would notice if you didn't pay back the money? Or that I'd forget?"

Dusty looked back, steadfastly trying to keep his insides from turning to jelly.

"Do you think I'm stupid? Is that it?" the Grub demanded, his voice rising in volume.

Not knowing how to respond, Dusty remained quiet.

"What am I going to do with you, Dusty? You borrow my hard-earned money and assure me you'll pay it back…"

The Grub leaned in close and grabbed Dusty's hair, pulling back hard. Dusty's head jerked back and he found himself looking almost straight up. He could see the faces of the two big men behind him.

The Grub's face was just inches from Dusty's right ear. "Thirty-five thousand dollars of my hard-earned money!" he bellowed.

Dusty resisted the urge to rub his ear despite the fact that it was ringing from the noise. But he knew rubbing it wouldn't help matters. Not now anyway.

The Grub just stared at him, as if pondering his options. Then he relaxed a bit, having made a decision. "I'm gonna do you a solid. You have three days until your loan is due in full. You'll pay back every penny you borrowed, plus interest, or I'm gonna start busting kneecaps! Do I make myself clear, Burns? Do I?"

His voice rose in intensity with every sentence until he was screaming.

One of the big men grinned sadistically down at Dusty. He felt a moment of panic rise up in him, but he forced himself to stay calm and tried to nod despite the pressure on his hair.

"In three days, you'll owe me fifty thousand," the Grub continued. "I want it delivered to me here at my office at 9:00 a.m. You do know where that is, don't you?"

With a sneer, he released Dusty's hair.

Dusty nodded more freely this time. He had a big knot in his throat and didn't trust his voice not to sound like a girl's.

"Show him a sample of what he can look forward to if he doesn't pay me," the Grub said to his goons. "Drop him off at home after."

Dusty's chair was suddenly spun sideways and a huge fist slammed into the side of his mouth. Pain exploded in his head and everything went dark.

• • •

When he came to, his good friends Charlie and Tina were peering down at him with concern on their faces.

"Where am I?" Dusty croaked, his throat dry.

"At home," they said in unison.

"How'd I get here?"

"We came over just in time to see you get tossed you of a car like a piece of discarded trash," Charlie replied.

Dusty groaned. "Why does my head hurt?"

"You banged your head when you were pushed out of the car," Tina said.

"Your apartment keys were still in your pocket, so we fished them out and dragged you inside," Charlie added. "Good thing you had them on you, but I hope we never have to do that again. It was difficult carrying your limp body all the way up here..." He looked down at his friend with concern. "Who were those guys who threw you out of the car?"

"Probably the Grub's boys."

"He wants his money, doesn't he." Tina said it like a statement.

Dusty gingerly touched the side of his face. His lip felt a bit swollen, but other than that everything felt fine albeit a bit tender to the touch.

"I told you not to borrow money from him," Charlie yelled, his face red. "We loaned you money so you wouldn't have to!"

"I know, I know, but I was running out of your money. And I couldn't find a job as a forklift operator even though I'm trained and my certification is up to date."

Dusty had been running a pet-dating service that ate up money faster than it came in. The whole idea was that people who had dogs or cats could come find a date for their pet if it was lonely.

"I told you this wouldn't work in Edmonton. Vancouver, maybe. But come on... Edmonton?" Tina smacked the side of her head. "What was I thinking when I agreed to go in on this?"

"It's not like I can default on the loan or declare bankruptcy," Dusty said, barely hearing her. "Guys like the Grub care more about their image than money. Oh sure, he likes the money too, which is why he's given me three days to come up with it. Three days! How is that going to help when in four years I haven't ever broken even? There's no way I can pay back the entire loan, all fifty thousand, in three days."

But if he didn't pay it back, the Grub would feel obligated to make an example out of him, to make sure others didn't get the idea that it was okay to borrow from him without paying it back.

What was he going to do?

CHAPTER
SIX

CRACKERS STARED AT HIS THREE fellow bank robbers: Jackson Tate, Peter Grimsby, and Vi Scarby.

Vi broke the silence. "When are we getting our money?" she asked impatiently.

Crackers looked at the woman. She was beautiful but cold and deadly. "Patience, Vi—"

"What's my cut?" Grimsby interrupted.

Grimsby didn't look like much. He had once been an accountant until he was caught embezzling from the Fortune 500 company he worked for. He'd lost his job, and his wife and kids had left him.

Of course, Crackers thought of him as fat... but he wasn't, not really. His body was like steel under his clothes. His appearance was deceptive.

"You get $1.2 million," Crackers said. "Same as everyone else."

"It should be $1.25 million," Vi pointed out.

"Brilliant, Vi. Except I planned the whole thing and provided the masks, shotguns, and coats which I had stored after our last job. So you each donate fifty grand to me, giving me $1.4 million. Any objections?"

After thinking a moment, they all shook their heads.

"But when do we get our money?" Vi asked again.

Jackson rested his massive arms on the table and smiled.

"What are you so happy about?" Vi asked him, sounding slightly irritated.

"I'm just content to wait until the heat is off to get our money," Jackson said. "I'm not in a hurry, like you are, to go back to jail."

Vi stood up and began to pace the room. "I don't want to go back to prison!"

"Ether consciously or subconsciously, you do," Crackers told her. "You don't realize it yet. But if I gave you your share now, it wouldn't be long before you were out spending it. The police would follow the money trail and catch you. So by your actions it would be clear that you *are* in a hurry to go back to jail. Those who aren't in a hurry to return to prison can wait forever. That being said, we'll get our shares when the heat dies down."

"Then by all means," Vi said, "hold onto my money and let me know when it's safe to divvy it up."

CHAPTER
SEVEN

DUSTY WAS ALL PACKED AND ready to go. He was leaving town and expected Charlie and Tina to pick him up any minute.

He just needed to make one stop—to the dentist's office. When the Grub's goon had punched him in the side of the mouth, he'd done some damage. One of his teeth hurt and Dusty needed it checked out before he could leave town. Then to the bus station and away from the Grub until he had the money to pay him back.

He knew the Grub wouldn't stop looking for him until the loan was paid back or until Dusty's knees were broken, so he had to disappear. That way he'd keep his kneecaps intact.

The money was due tomorrow at 9:00 a.m. He was sure the Grub's people would be keeping an eye on him as the deadline grew closer. If he didn't leave now, he might not get the chance.

He took one last look around his second story apartment. Two suitcases stood packed and ready by the door.

Then he saw his wallet-sized forklift license on the dresser and decided to take it with him. Picking it up, he removed his wallet from his back pocket and slid the license inside.

Looking around, Dusty decided that the furniture would stay. He wouldn't miss any of it. He'd gotten all of it secondhand and it hadn't been in the best shape when he'd moved in four years ago, when he'd started his new business venture.

He was paid up until the end of the month, three and a half weeks away. But he didn't think he'd be back to pay next month's rent.

He looked at his watch: 9:40 a.m.

Where are those guys? My dental appointment is at ten. Dusty had tried to get in first thing in the morning, but they hadn't been able to see him any earlier.

He heard a car door slam on the street below and looked out the window to spy Charlie and Tina. Tina was just starting to get out of the car, with Charlie coming around the front of the vehicle towards the apartment building.

Dusty turned away from the window, grabbed his bags, and left his apartment, locking the door behind him. He walked quickly and decided to take the stairs. Much faster than the elevator.

He pushed open the door with his back and bounded down the stairs with a suitcase in each hand. When he burst out of the door at the bottom, he almost collided with Charlie in the foyer.

"Whoa, boy! Where's the fire?" Charlie asked.

"Let's go," Dusty said. "My appointment is at ten o'clock! Why isn't the trunk open?"

"It's full." At Dusty's raised eyebrow, Charlie added, "It's a long story. Throw your bags in the back seat and hop in. We'll explain later."

Dusty opened the rear door, threw his bags in, and jumped in after them. Once Tina and Charlie had gotten back in the vehicle, they took off for the dental office downtown with Charlie at the wheel.

"Can you drive any faster?" Dusty said. "I'm going to be late."

Tina turned around in her seat, laughing. "I've never seen anyone in such a rush to get to the dentist!"

• • •

Fifteen minutes later, Dusty was sitting in the dental office's waiting room reading a women's magazine. It was the only thing available.

While reading the magazine, he began thinking of his Aunt Mae, his mother's sister. She had been a positive influence in his life and had always helped him however she could, including having him come to visit in the summers when his parents were both working. Plus she had sated his appetite for chocolate by never failing to send him some on those holidays when chocolates were prevalent. Easter and Christmas for sure. He'd have to give her a call when everything with the Grub was over.

The receptionist popped up behind her counter. "Dusty Burns?"

"Yes?" Dusty said, looking up from the magazine.

"You may come in now."

He followed her into the examination room.

"Please sit down," she said. "The dentist will be with you shortly."

Dusty sat in the dental chair while she fitted a small bib on him.

"If you want to watch TV, use this." She handed him a remote.

He was busy flipping through channels when the dentist entered the room. The man wore surgical gloves and a facemask. He sat on the stool and rolled over to Dusty, lowering the back of Dusty's chair.

"Now open wide and let's take a look." The dentist slid a mirror and a tool with a sharp end into Dusty's open mouth. "You have a toothache, is that right?"

"Uuuh-huuuh."

"Now which side hurts?"

"'ight 'ide"

"Okay, right side. Let's take a peek."

The dentist poked several teeth with the sharp tool, then removed the implement. "Okay, I think I found the problem. You have a bruise on your gum... feels like a toothache to you, but it's only your gums. It'll clear up on its own. If you'd like to speed up the healing process, though, try swishing salt water in your mouth once or twice a day. I can give you something for the pain if you'd like."

"That would be nice," Dusty said.

"Drop your pants and bend over," the dentist instructed while getting off his stool and heading across the room.

"Pardon me?"

For a moment, Dusty was confused. Dentists didn't give people shots in their posterior. Did they? He hadn't gone to see his doctor by mistake, had he?

Dusty took a closer look around the room—the dental chair, dentist tools, a set of large fake teeth... Nope, he was at the dentist all right.

The dentist turned around with a large needle in his hands. He flicked the end while depressing the plunger a tiny bit. A squirt of liquid came out the tip.

"I need you to get off the chair, Mr. Burns. That's right. Now drop your pants and bend over."

Dusty stared at him dumbly. His brain seemed frozen, like a deer in headlights. Like most things with him, this just wasn't sinking in.

The dentist flicked the needle a couple more times. Why did he want to stick that needle in him?

Dusty turned and charged for the door, the dentist right behind him. He ran out of the dental office with his heart in his throat and headed for the stairs.

Just as he ran past the elevator, the doors opened and he saw two big goons inside. When they spotted him, they joined in the chase.

All four of them entered the stairwell, Dusty just a couple of steps ahead. He flew down the stairs and widened the gap a bit, then burst through the door at the bottom and headed for the street. His legs pumped as fast as he could make them as he gasped for air and willed his body to run faster.

"Wait," the dentist yelled as he burst out of the building. "I have something to give you before you leave!"

Dusty sprinted across the large cement expanse. He spotted his friends leaning on the front of the car parked at the curb. They were talking together and hadn't noticed him yet.

"Start the car!" Dusty yelled.

He looked back and saw the dentist followed by the two goons still hot on his trail. They were slightly further back than the last time Dusty had checked.

Tina jumped off the hood and ran around to her door. Charlie got off the car, flipped the back door open, then hopped into the front seat and started the car. Tina slid in.

Dusty dove into the back seat, then sat up quickly to shut and lock his door. "Go, go, go!"

CHAPTER
EIGHT

CHARLIE TURNED THE STEERING WHEEL and floored the gas pedal. The tires smoked and they were off. If they could make it to the highway without being spotted, they had a good chance of eluding these men.

As Dusty looked back, he saw the goons change direction and run for a big black car parked at the curb. It was a dark blue Cadillac Deville. The dentist had gone back up to his office.

"They're getting in their car!" Dusty called out, his voice thick with fear. "How on earth did they know I had a dental appointment?"

They zigzagged a bit as they headed south, turning left and right as often as they could. Finally, after a few blocks, when the other car wasn't gaining, Dusty's heart stopped beating like a jackhammer. He started to calm down.

"Maybe I should go back and hand out business cards," Dusty said.

"What business cards?" Charlie asked, his eyes on the road in front of him.

"You know, for my pet-dating business."

"Are you nuts? Don't you know who those goons work for?" Dusty didn't answer, forcing Tina to answer her own question. "Those are the Grub's men."

"You can't be sure of that," Dusty said weakly.

When Tina turned and glared at Dusty like he was an idiot, he slumped back in the seat.

Suddenly Charlie turned left. He then took another quick left into a parking lot and drove behind a fast food restaurant and turned the engine off.

"Let's sit here out of sight for a few minutes and hope they cruise right by," Charlie said.

The car had barely come to standstill when Tina hopped out. "Be right back!"

A few minutes later she returned with hamburgers, fries, and milkshakes for everyone.

"What's that for?" Dusty asked while licking his lips.

"I just had a feeling we were going to need this."

Charlie started the car and headed back to the road. The coast was clear, so he turned into traffic and they drove towards the bus terminal.

"I'll give you yours when we get to the terminal," Tina told him, smiling. "But Charlie and I may be playing tag with these guys for a while yet. That's why I got food for us too. Hopefully we can get you on the bus, then head off and lead these goons on a merry chase."

Dusty raised his eyebrow. "But you guys will be putting yourselves in danger! I got into this... let me get out of this on my own."

"Not a chance, buddy!" Charlie looked at him in the rearview mirror. "We're friends and friends help each other."

Charlie cruised along at the speed limit so as not to attract any attention. Just as they were about to take the final turn towards the terminal, however, a dark blue sedan turned off a side street and fell in behind them.

The hairs on the back of Dusty's neck stood up as Charlie swung back into traffic and accelerated.

"How did they find us?" Tina asked to no one in particular.

"We need to figure out what direction to go," Charlie said.

"I think the Grub will expect us to drive to a big city—say, Vancouver," Dusty mused. "And if he doesn't find us there, I think he'll look south, maybe to Calgary or somewhere in the U.S."

"Then let's go west, as he expects. And once we know we've lost them, we'll take a road heading back east."

"Okay, but where will we go?"

"Toronto?" Tina interjected.

Charlie shook his head. "Nope."

"Montreal?" Dusty asked.

"The Maritimes?"

"Winnipeg?"

"No, no, and no," Charlie said.

Dusty seemed confused. "What else is there?"

"Exactly. That's what the Grub will wonder. So we'll go to Saskatchewan. He'll never think of looking for us there."

CHAPTER
NINE

THEY WHIPPED AROUND THE CORNER, gravel spitting behind them like a twin stream of mad bees. The engine growled as they flew along the back road heading west, looking for an opportunity to turn south and then east.

When they hit a rise in the road, the sound of the engine rose to a frenzied pitch. The wheels caught air, but on they drove, rounding curves at breakneck speed, up hills and down, the roadside flashing past them.

As Tina studied the map on her lap, Dusty wondered how she could read with the car bouncing so much.

Eventually they came upon a paved highway that headed south. There were no cars on the road and the pavement was dry, with thick groves of trees lining the way on either side. The road was pretty straight for a while, so Tina passed around the food she'd bought. Dusty ate hungrily as they continued on, all the while trying to imagine how he would raise fifty thousand dollars.

"They're back!" Charlie hollered.

Dusty jerked as he was reaching for his milkshake and spied the now-familiar Cadillac coming up behind them fast.

Suddenly Charlie, Tina, and Dusty were thrown back into their seats.

"Did they just ram us?" Tina gasped.

Charlie was too busy trying to keep the car on the road to answer. When they were rammed again, their vehicle slewed left towards the ditch.

If we hit that ditch at this speed, there's no way we'll stop before reaching the trees, Dusty thought.

Charlie fought hard, using all his driving skill to bring the car out of its sideways slide and get it under control. He finally got the car heading straight again and picked up some of the speed he'd just lost.

But the Cadillac quickly started to catch up.

"What do they have under the hood of that thing?" Charlie wondered aloud. "They shouldn't be able to catch us so easily."

The Cadillac pulled alongside them and slammed into the side of their vehicle. Dusty could see one of the Grub's goons grinning at them from the front seat.

"Dusty! Throw your milkshake onto their windshield," Tina hollered.

Charlie hit the brakes and dropped back. The Cadillac also braked, and just when they did he stomped on the gas and surged ahead of them.

"Now!" Charlie hollered.

Dusty had already lowered his window in anticipation of this, so he tossed out his milkshake ahead of the Cadillac. The wind caught it and slammed it back right onto the windshield, splattering it all over.

"That should make it tough for them to see," Dusty said.

The Cadillac fell back, its windshield wipers going full blast while the car swerved around, losing speed.

Charlie accelerated and soon left them behind.

Within a few minutes the scenery started to change and the road turned downhill. At the bottom of the hill, a bridge crossed the North Saskatchewan River. They were almost to the end of the bridge when the dark blue Caddy came roaring down the hill at high speed and caught them just as the road began to climb uphill again.

Charlie gunned it as they started up the hill. When a second lane opened up to the right, the goons pulled up alongside again. They pointed to the ditch and grinned.

Suddenly Charlie hammered the brakes and they dropped back. Before the goons could respond, Charlie swung over so the right tip of the bumper was positioned right behind their bumper. Then he hit the gas and the front of the Cadillac swung to the right down the embankment and hit a stand of trees at the bottom.

Tina looked back as the car surged ahead. "They're getting out. They seem okay, but their car isn't going anywhere any time soon."

"They'll probably call in some backup, so we'd better get off this road when we can," Dusty pointed out.

They stuck to the back roads and headed around the southern end of Pigeon Lake, then headed east a bit before reconnecting to Highway 2, heading south. That's when Charlie really opened the car up to top speed.

They'd only travelled about an hour before another big black car showed up in the rearview mirror. There was nothing to be seen on this stretch of highway but the occasional farmhouse.

They got off the highway and once more took side roads. The car sped along, its engine whining as they hit every bump and screamed around every corner. Charlie went through small towns and doubled back.

Finally they ended up in one small town around the supper hour, the black car still following them. Charlie came to rest at a stop sign for three full seconds, then turned right and quickly accelerated. The men in the black car blew right through the intersection... but before they could get far, a siren sounded and a police car came roaring out of a side street.

"How did you know that would happen?" Dusty asked as he watched the black car get pulled over.

Charlie grinned. "I caught a glimpse of a car hiding in the shadows just as we pulled to a stop. I had a hunch it was a police car. Those guys will be tied up for twenty minutes at least." But his smile soon vanished. "I just don't understand how they keep finding us. We took so many of those gravel backroads, and even these secondary highways which don't look like they get much traffic. I'm thinking they put a tracker on my car. It's the only thing that makes sense."

"We have to find someplace to stop so we can find and destroy it," Tina said. "Let me see where we are on the map."

A few minutes later, she let out a big whoop.

"Found it! We'll be coming to an intersection in a few kilometers and there's a town just a bit to the east."

Within a few miles they came to the intersection and turned left. Soon they came to another, this one next to a gas station with an attached convenience store and restaurant. The town itself wasn't visible yet, but they figured it was most likely a few minutes south of here.

Charlie pulled in, drove past the gas pumps, and disappeared around the far side of the building to keep out of sight.

Immediately the middle-aged man who manned the gas pumps rushed over to them. "You can't park there!" he hollered.

Tina was in no mood for this. She bounced out of the car as if she had a bee in her pants. "Can't? Did you just say we can't park here?" she said, running up to the attendant. "*Can't* means we aren't able to park here... so I ask you, does it look like we were able to park here? Does the car not look parked to you? I think you meant to say we *shouldn't* park here." She put her hands on her hips.

The gas attendant just opened and closed his mouth like a fish. No words came out.

Charlie and Dusty got out of the car and watched Tina for a few minutes.

Boy, this guy is in for it, Dusty thought.

"Come help me look for this tracking device," Charlie said quietly to him. "Run your hands around the wheel wells and I'll crawl underneath the car and take a look."

"Why is she so upset?" Dusty asked in curiosity as they got to work. "Can't, shouldn't... what's the difference?"

"Her father is an English major and he corrected her English incessantly growing up," his friend told him. "It really gets under her skin when others make mistakes like that."

It took ten minutes, but finally Charlie found the tracker. It was a small thing, stuck to the side of the exhaust pipe.

As soon as it was located, Charlie walked over to the gas pumps and unobtrusively placed the tracker in a wheel well of one of the trucks sitting there. The gas attendant was busy filling its gas tank while still being lectured by Tina on his choice of words.

Dusty kept a lookout, and it seemed to him that neither the attendant nor the driver of the truck saw Charlie plant the bug.

While walking back to the car, Charlie caught Tina's eye.

She stopped mid-speech. "Fine! We'll move the car, if that's what it will take to make you happy!"

She stomped off back to the car, with Charlie smiling right behind her.

All three piled into the car and backed out. But before hitting the road and heading south, they gassed the car up.

"We'll head south a bit further before turning east," Charlie suggested. "Just in case the Grub has more of his guys out patrolling for us."

They rolled into Medicine Hat several hours later and found a motel where they could park the car around back, out of sight of anyone passing by. The Hat, as the locals called it, was a decent size and there were enough hotels and motels that Dusty didn't think the Grub's men would find them even if they ended up in the same city.

Dusty hadn't been sleeping well since his meeting with the loan shark. In the morning he woke up still tired, then took a shower and put on fresh clothes.

As he zipped up his suitcase, he heard a knock at his door.

"Dusty? You up yet?" Charlie called.

He grabbed his suitcase, then carried it to the door and opened it. "Are we ready to go?" he asked his friend.

"You bet. Bring your suitcase to the car and we'll see if we can get it to fit. We already have your other suitcase in there."

"When you picked me up yesterday, you said your trunk was full. What is it full of?"

Charlie was already walking towards the car. "Come and see for yourself."

Dusty carried his suitcase down to the car which was parked outside Charlie's room.

Charlie opened the trunk and Dusty saw more suitcases and bags. "Whose are those?"

"Mostly Tina's."

"Wait, what? Why does Tina have her luggage in your trunk?"

"I have a bag in there too," Charlie said.

Dusty leaned against the trunk of the car. "I'd like to hear why you both brought bags. I can't believe I didn't notice this last night."

"You were pretty out of it. We packed because we felt something was going to happen and all three us would end up on the run."

"Fair enough," Dusty told him. "But you can just drop me at the closest bus station. There's no need for both of you to disappear with me."

"Oh no," said Tina as she came out of her room, right beside Charlie's. "You aren't leaving us behind. We're in this together now. We're sticking with you."

Dusty looked at Charlie, who nodded in agreement.

"But what about your jobs?" Dusty asked. "You can't just leave them behind."

Tina sighed. "I have a lot of vacation time saved up. So I'm officially on vacation."

"And I got laid off a few days ago, so I'm in between jobs," Charlie said. "I have ample savings, though. I'm good to go."

Dusty raised his hands in surrender. "Okay then. Let's get back on the road."

After checking out, they headed east along the Trans-Canada Highway, so named because it stretched from coast to coast 7,821 kilometers, or 4,860 miles. Dusty hoped their pursuers thought they were still going south, heading for the U.S. border.

At some point when he wasn't paying attention, they entered Saskatchewan. And a few hours later they came to Moose Jaw. From there, they turned north towards Saskatoon.

Dusty finally relaxed, knowing that there was no way those black Cadillacs would find them now. His head slowly lowered to his chest and he fell asleep.

Suddenly the car hit a bump in the road and caught a bit of air before settling back on the surface. The struts groaned under the pressure.

Dusty's head snapped up. "Bump!"

Tina just shook her head. "Such a moron..."

By this time, Dusty didn't have a clue where they were.

As dusk approached, he fell asleep again, and when he awoke some hours later the car was parked on the side street of an unfamiliar town. Charlie and Tina weren't in the car.

He got out on stiff legs and opened the front door to pop the trunk. When he opened it, he didn't see anything. Charlie's bag was gone, as were Tina's. Dusty's bags were gone too. The trunk was empty and there was no sign of the car keys.

CHAPTER

TEN

DUSTY LOOKED AROUND AND REALIZED there wasn't much to see. In the dark he noticed some nondescript buildings that were probably warehouses. One building close by looked more like a small office perhaps. It had some exterior lights on.

He headed closer, and after a few steps his legs felt less stiff. He spotted a sign but couldn't read it until he got right under it: Duggan Printing. Why would a printing company be open so late? A rush job?

Oh well. Maybe someone inside would know where Charlie and Tina had disappeared to.

The outer door opened easily. Inside the light was dim, but he could see well enough. He spotted a set of double doors with light visible underneath.

He pushed one door open and stopped in surprise. He had expected to see printing presses spitting out pages of paper with people running back and forth. Instead he saw men in tuxedos and women in beautiful dresses dancing in a well-lit room.

Dusty stepped inside, blinking against the bright lights, trying to understand what he was seeing. He suddenly noticed that everyone was staring at him and he realized how out of place he must look in his well-worn jeans, T-shirt, and running shoes.

He looked around for Charles and Tina but couldn't find them. Among the dancers were a well-dressed bride and groom in the middle of the room.

Near the back wall, he saw a short, wiry old man making eye contact with him. The white-haired man suddenly turned and disappeared from view. He'd had a sinister appearance, wearing a nasty sneer. The expression on his face made Dusty shiver involuntarily.

When Dusty reached the back wall, he could see that there was a hallway back there. No one was to the left, but the right hallway curved away; he figured the creepy man had gone that direction.

A little way down the right hallway, he came to a door with a small window in it just below eye level. The window had bars in it.

Dusty bent over a bit and peered through the bars to spot a bed with a small table and chair. He tried the door but it found it locked.

Each room Dusty looked into was similarly empty, although in addition to the spartan furniture some had a toilet. But he saw no sign of anyone.

The further down the hall he went, the more he felt chills run up and down his spine. He felt like he was being watched despite not seeing anyone around.

Halfway down the hall, he turned and fled back toward the room with the dance floor. Only now there was no one there, either.

He practically ran back to the front entrance. He opened the door and stepped out into the cool night air, taking big calming breaths. How had everyone from the dance floor disappeared so fast?

Dusty wondered if he'd been exploring that hallway longer than he thought. The most important thing now was to find Charlie and Tina.

CHAPTER
ELEVEN

DUSTY SPIED SOME LIGHTER SKY to the north, likely the result of lit-up buildings, and hoped he would find a motel in that direction.

He set off, and several minutes later he spied something up ahead. Not a motel, but a gas station with all its lights on. He walked past a payphone and up to the double glass doors. Inside, a young man stood behind the counter of the convenience store.

Dusty didn't want to appear like an idiot and ask what town this was—and based on the sign of that printing place, he thought he would make a guess that it was called Duggan. But since he wasn't positive, he decided to ask for a map.

"You got a map for this town?" he asked, noticing that the man had a nametag with *Steve* written on it.

"Which town?" Steve asked.

"This town."

Steve rooted behind the counter for a minute but came up empty. "I might have one in the back. Nobody really asks for them anymore. But I'm not allowed to leave the counter unmanned."

"I'll watch it for you," Dusty offered.

"I don't know you. How do I know I can trust you?"

"All I really need is a motel that's clean and affordable. Can you point me in the right direction?"

Steve pointed out the door towards the road.

"Is the motel on this road?" Dusty asked.

"I think it's a hotel, but yeah. It's one block off the main road."

"Hotel, motel... what's the difference?"

"With motels, you park right outside your door," Steve explained. "No interior hallways. With hotels, as far as I understand it, the access to the rooms is all inside."

"Fair enough. What's the name of the side street where the hotel is?"

Steve shrugged. "I could find it on a map."

Dusty raised his eyebrows inquiringly.

"Okay, okay... I'll go look for the map," the man said. "Just stay here on that side of the counter. If any customers come in, tell them I'll be right back."

Dusty nodded as Steve disappeared into a back room.

After a moment Dusty realized he was very hungry. He spied a warmer with hotdogs just behind the counter. To get to them, he would have to disobey the clerk's instructions...

Feeling his stomach growl, he decided to chance it. He got a hotdog, stuffed it in a bun, and squeezed some mustard and ketchup on it.

He went back to the other side of the counter and ate, all the while hearing sounds of a commotion from the back room.

Dusty finished his hotdog and wondered what was taking Steve so long. He was about to go see how the kid was faring when all the rummaging sounds finally ceased. Then the door to the back room opened and Steve emerged, looking like he'd just come through a whirlwind. His uniform was in disarray, his hair disheveled, with dust on his shirt but a victorious grin on his face and a map clutched in his hand.

Steve slapped the map down on the counter. "That will be two dollars."

Dusty picked up the map, unfolded it, and placed it flat on the counter. "Show me where this motel is."

Steve turned the map around, picked up a pen, and looked at the map for a moment before circling one of the intersections. "The gas station is here."

He then drew a straight line from the circled area to another intersection three blocks away, indicated a left turn, and made a circle with the word "Hotel" written above it.

Dusty leaned over and studied the map. The directions seemed easy enough.

When he straightened up, Steve was staring at him. "Is that mustard on your face?"

Dusty dabbed at the corner of his mouth. "I had a hotdog while you were looking in the back room."

"I thought I told you not to come behind the counter?"

"How else was I supposed to get myself some food? I was starving and you were gone a long time. Add the cost of the hotdog to the map. Now what do I owe you?"

"You weren't going to tell me, were you?" Steve said.

"Yes I was. I wanted you to mark the map first. I was going to tell you when I paid, but you didn't give me a chance."

Steve nodded as if accepting Dusty's explanation. "Six bucks."

Dusty dug in his pocket, counted out the money, and handed it over.

Steve folded up the map and gave it to Dusty.

"It's been a pleasure," Dusty said. He picked up the map, turned, and walked out the door.

● ● ●

Ten minutes later, Dusty stepped through the front door of a small, well-kept hotel. Once inside he could heard the clink of cutlery and the murmur of voices. He noticed a dining room off to his left but walked past it and continued to the front desk.

No one waited behind the counter, so he rang the bell set conveniently on top. A moment later, a man and women emerged from a side door.

Dusty turned his head and took them both in. The man was bald, wore glasses perched on his nose, and had the biggest smile Dusty had ever seen. He had a thick body but looked to be fit and had a spring in his step. The woman had white hair and also wore glasses; she was slim and seemed a bit frail, but there was strength in her gaze. They both looked to be around fifty, although with her having white hair maybe they were a bit older. He wasn't sure.

"What can we do for you, young man? I'm Tom and this is my lovely wife Wendy."

Dusty didn't think it possible, but when Tom introduced his wife his smile got even bigger.

"I'm looking to get a room," Dusty said.

"And how long will you need a room for?" Tom asked.

Dusty scratched his chin, thinking. "I'm not really sure. You see, my friends have gone missing and I'll need to stay here for at least as long as it takes to find them."

"We for sure have a room for you. It's the least we can do to help," Tom said gently. Wendy stood behind him, taking this all in and nodding her head to everything her husband said.

"How much per night for a basic room?" Dusty asked.

"We charge forty dollars a night."

Dusty raised his eyebrows. "That's it?" He'd never in his life paid less than a hundred dollars per night.

"This isn't some big city, young fellow. Prices are more reasonable in out-of-the-way places like this. But if you want to pay more, we won't stop you." Tom's eyes twinkled.

Dusty plunked forty dollars on the counter and suddenly Wendy came alive. She turned and, with deliberation, picked a key from the key rack. She came out from behind the counter.

"If you'll just follow me," she said.

Wendy led Dusty around the corner and down a hallway before stopping at a door and opening it for him.

He walked past her into the room and saw a double bed, a television, and in the corner a small table and two chairs.

"There are fresh towels in the bathroom," Wendy said behind him. "The remote for the TV is on the dresser. Local calls are free. The dining room is still open, but the kitchen will be closing in thirty minutes if you're hungry. If you need anything, please let us know."

And then she was gone, the door closing.

Dusty looked at his watch. 9:30 p.m. Suddenly he wondered if the time was the same as it was back in Edmonton. He looked around the room and spied a digital alarm clock on the far side of the bed, resting on a stand. He was happy to see that it read the same time as his watch.

His stomach rumbled and Dusty headed out to see what food the restaurant had.

Forty minutes later, Dusty was just finishing up the last of his steak and potatoes with baby spinach and melted butter when Tom and Wendy came by his table.

"We've been thinking, young man, that we'd like to help in any way we can in this quest for your missing friends," Tom said.

"Anything at all," Wendy chimed in.

Tom nodded. "If I may, I'd like to offer some helpful advice, Mr. Burns."

"Call me Dusty, please."

"Of course, Dusty! Now, since you have no luggage and you're staying until you find your friends, it stands to reason that you'll need clothes and some incidentals. There is a good men's store on Main Street. The owner runs the place and the prices are decent. The drugstore is a couple doors down and you can get a toothbrush, toothpaste, razors, shaving cream, a comb… things like that."

"And if we can help in finding your friends, don't hesitate to ask," Wendy piped up. "Ooh, I just love a good adventure!"

CHAPTER
TWELVE

DUSTY HAD A LEISURELY BREAKFAST of eggs and toast in the morning, and once he was finished he paid his bill and headed back into the main foyer of the hotel. Tom was behind the registration desk, so Dusty sauntered over to chat.

"Good day, young fellow!" Tom said when he caught sight of Dusty.

"Hi Tom. Is that offer to help find my friends still open?"

Tom closed what looked like an accounting book and pushed his glances up onto the top of his bald head. "Of course. What can I help you with?"

Dusty explained about the wedding he'd stumbled upon. "I'm just wondering if you might have a newspaper which would have a list of any weddings that took place yesterday."

"I believe I do. Come, follow me and we'll look. Can you tell me anything about the building where you saw this wedding?"

Dusty described the building. "The sign out front said Duggan Printing."

"Yes, yes, I know the place. I don't know who owns it, though."

Tom led Dusty behind the door to their own quarters and pulled a newspaper off the desk in the corner. He flipped to the classifieds. "Ah, this should be the one we need."

The man placed the paper on a tabletop and found the section reserved for wedding announcements, running his finger down the column.

"There aren't many," Tom said. "The first two give the location, and neither one is the place you were at. Hmm, this one sounds possible. Hank Clyde Thomas and Wendy Sophia Norman. That's strange. There's no picture of the couple and no location for the wedding."

"Can I keep that?" Dusty asked.

"Of course!" Tom tore out the section. When he handed it over, Dusty saw that he had torn out the entire wedding announcement section.

"One other thing," Dusty said. "Could you point me in the direction of the police station? I have a map of Duggan in my room. If you give me a minute, I'll get it and you can show me where everything is."

"No need. I have maps at the front counter with everything labelled. Come with me." Tom hesitated a moment. "By the way, the town's name is pronounced *Doogan*."

Dusty followed him to the front counter. Tom reached under the counter and pulled out a pad with colorful maps.

"Here is the police station, and Main Street." Tom produced a pen and marked an x on the main road. "This is where you'll find the men's store I mentioned last night, and the drugstore will be two doors down."

Dusty took the map, folded it, and slid it into his back pocket. He then paid for another night before heading out of the hotel to find the police station and see what they could do to help him find his friends.

It took less than twenty minutes for him to find the station and walk into the cool, dimly lit interior. A man in a sergeant's uniform sat behind the front desk reading some papers in front of him.

He looked up when Dusty entered and raised his eyebrows expectantly.

Dusty explained what had happened to him, how he'd woken up in the car after driving here with his friends having disappeared.

"When did this happen?" the sergeant asked.

"Last night."

"So you expect foul play, do you?" The sergeant sounded rather condescending.

"Either that or kidnapping," Dusty replied, feeling a bit irritated at the sergeant's surly attitude.

"Foul play includes the possibility of kidnapping. They disappeared last night, you say?"

"That's what I just said. Can you help me find them?" Dusty was starting to get tired of the sergeant's attitude.

Maybe he's just having a bad day.

"How do I know you didn't have something to do with it?" A hint of a smile tugged at the corners of the sergeant's mouth, like he enjoyed giving people a hard time.

Dusty looked at his nametag: *Ted Larsen.*

He was still looking at Dusty as if he expected a response, but Dusty had no intention of answering such a biased question.

After a pause, Larsen kept talking. "We can check the local hotels, check our reports of hospitals for the last twelve hours, and see if any John Does showed up. But to do that you'll need to fill out a lot of paperwork and they have to be missing for at least twenty-four hours. Why don't you look around town today and check back with us tomorrow?"

Dusty stared at Larsen, thinking it would be better if the missing persons forms got filled out now and he got some help looking for his friends. He didn't have any idea where they might be and didn't know the town. But he could tell from the look on the man's face that no help would be forthcoming, at least not on this day.

He turned to leave, and as he did so a couple of other officers entered.

"Hi Squid!" one of them called as he approached the desk where Larsen worked.

Dusty caught Larsen glaring at the other officers. *At least it's not just me he doesn't like.*

As Dusty left, he smiled. So Sergeant Ted Larsen was known as Squid Larsen. Suddenly he was looking forward to coming back.

He headed back to the same gas station he'd been at the night before, wanting to see if the phone booth he'd seen there had a phone book.

He was relieved when he got there and saw that it did. But unfortunately a man was currently in the booth engaged in a spirited discussion, judging from his animated hand gestures. So Dusty sat on the curb by the side of the gas station and leaned against the wall.

He was almost nodding off when the fellow slammed down the receiver and stormed out of the booth, walking over to an older convertible and driving off with squealing tires.

Dusty stepped into the booth and tried to prop open the phone book while he pulled out the newspaper page and looked for a name: Hank Thomas. He located it and took note of the man's address, which wasn't far away.

When he found the address, he found an empty lot. The address he had been given was located between two properties. The lot was definitely the right place, but it was obviously a fake address.

Dusty mulled over the situation. The newly married couple obviously didn't live here, yet they had listed this place as their address. It made no sense. Were they involved in the disappearance of Charlie and Tina? If not, why had they given a bogus address?

Dusty sat down on the curb and tried to think of how to find the recently married couple. He couldn't seem to come up with anything.

When he checked his watch, it was nearing noon. He went back to the hotel by a different route, trying to see as much of the town as he could. Along the way he passed a small, friendly-looking restaurant called the First Street Diner. He hoped they served a good cup of coffee. He also located a bank and a laundromat.

But that was for another time. He wanted to explore more, but his stomach was growling.

Lunch back at the hotel was homecooked and the best food Dusty had eaten in some time: thick, freshly made bread and mouthwatering stew to dip his bread in. While he ate he started thinking about the events that had brought him to this small town in Saskatchewan. He had a strong hunch that the wedding he'd stumbled upon and his missing friends were somehow connected.

Just then, Tom and Wendy arrived at his table.

Dusty looked up from his meal. "Care to join me?"

"We'd be delighted," Wendy said.

"To what do I owe the pleasure?" Dusty asked.

Tom smiled. "We just want to talk. We're curious what brought you to our town."

"That is, if you don't mind our asking," Wendy added.

Dusty hesitated, but then, much to his surprise, he realized that in the short time he'd known Tom and Wendy he had come to genuinely like and trust them. So he told them the story from the beginning.

"It's amazing you made it to Saskatchewan at all!" Wendy exclaimed.

"We'd like to help you out, young man," Tom said, changing the subject. "You know, with the room rate." He noticed the look of confusion on Dusty's face. "We're not comping your room. This isn't Vegas. We had something different in mind."

Now Dusty really was confused.

Tom hastened to explain. "I couldn't help but notice you didn't have a lot of money in your wallet when you paid us yesterday."

Dusty didn't know what to say to that. He was floored, to say the least. "You saw inside my wallet?" he stammered.

"I couldn't really help it. You opened up the wallet pretty wide, trying to find two twenties. Tell you what. You look for a job, and in the meantime we'll keep a tab for you. Now, don't get the idea we do this for everyone. We don't. But Wendy and I got to talking after she showed you to the room last night… You have no luggage, and no change of clothes. You'll need incidentals as well…" Tom leaned forward. "Have you been to the men's store I told you about?"

"Not yet. I was hoping to go this afternoon."

"Okay, good. The man who owns the store is an expert at picking out clothes that will look good on you."

CHAPTER
THIRTEEN

ONCE DUSTY FINISHED HIS MEAL, he settled his bill with the cashier and headed back to his room. There he grabbed the map, then went out the hotel's front door and headed into town. It wasn't a long walk, and before he knew it he was at the men's clothing store.

Stan, the owner, was well-dressed with silver hair and a friendly face. Dusty liked him immediately. The store seemed to have everything a man would wear, right down to undershirts.

Stan helped Dusty pick out a few shirts, some jeans, socks, underwear, and even a pair of dress shoes. Dusty also picked up a black dinner jacket along with a white shirt and black slacks. When the bill was rung up, the cost was far less than what Dusty had expected.

With bags in hand, Dusty walked down the sidewalk to see a bit more of the town. There was the public library, the courthouse, and plenty of offices for lawyers and accountants.

He had only wandered a couple of blocks when it started to rain. Dusty had been so intent on looking around that he hadn't noticed the clouds roll in.

Spotting the friendly-looking diner from earlier, he bolted for it and squeezed through the doorway with his bags in hand.

Dusty settled into one of the booths in the back of the restaurant and stowed his bags underneath the table. Then he leaned back and relaxed.

A moment later a waitress was at his side. "What can I get you, sir?"

The young woman had dark brown hair, soft brown eyes, and an engaging smile. She looked to be about his age.

"Please, just call me Dusty," he said. "I'm not into fancy titles."

She smiled a dazzling smile. "Sure, Dusty. What'll it be?"

"Just a coffee, please. One sugar, one cream."

"Coming right up!"

While he waited for his coffee, Dusty thought about Charles and Tina. Where could they be? Did that sinister old man he'd seen at the wedding have something to do with their disappearance?

He didn't have the answers. He just knew he needed to find his friends.

His coffee arrived and he took a grateful sip. He hadn't had a coffee all day and his body was craving one.

As he stared out the window, he noticed a man across the street sitting on a bench. It looked like the man was staring at him. He wore a light tan trench coat, his dark hair was plastered to his scalp in the rain and he wore glasses.

Surely it couldn't be one of the Grub's men, Dusty thought. *They couldn't have tracked me here already? Could they*?

Just then, someone slid into the seat opposite him. He looked up, a bit startled, and saw that it was just the waitress. When he saw her, he instantly forgot about the man across the street.

"Hi, I'm Cindy Lambert." She extended her hand for him to shake.

Dusty shook it, feeling a bit bewildered. "Dusty Burns. Do you sit down with all your customers?"

"Of course not, silly! It's just that you're alone and... well, you looked friendly. You don't mind, do you?" she ended a little breath-lessly.

"I don't mind. But doesn't your boss frown on you doing this?"

"There's no one else in here for me to serve, so my boss won't care. If no one is complaining, he's happy!" Cindy laughed. "Besides, I wanted to talk to you! I haven't seen you around before. Are you new in town?"

"Yes," he admitted. "I ended up here with two friends, but they've gone missing. I'm looking for them and hoping to find a job while I'm at it. Do you know any place that's hiring?"

"I might," she said with a twinkle in her eye. "What are you skilled at?"

"A number of things, but I thought I'd look for a job as a forklift driver."

"Are you qualified?" She had an easy way of talking that made Dusty feel completely relaxed around her.

"I have my certificate. I started driving one when I was sixteen."

"Excellent," she said, grinning. "I might know of something along those lines. I'll check for you. Now, what do you mean your friends are missing?"

"Whoa! I think it's time I got to ask you some questions, don't you?"

"What would you like to know about me?"

"How about telling me how long you've lived here?"

"I grew up here," she said.

"Do you work at this diner full-time?"

"I work thirty hours a week. Usually from lunch until six o'clock. Which is nice, since it gives me some free time during the week and I don't have to get up early."

"Let me guess, you're a night person and not working until noon fits right into your schedule."

Cindy laughed. "You guessed it. Now, are you going to tell me about your missing friends?"

"One more question. How old are you?"

"Twenty-two. And you?"

"Twenty-four."

She smiled broadly.

"Are you single?" Dusty asked.

"Hey, that's two questions!" Cindy winked. "I'll answer your second question after you tell me about your friends."

"You're right. Okay, I'll tell you."

Cindy had such an openness about her that Dusty found himself beginning to warm up to her.

Dusty explained about his failed business, running from the loan sharks, and falling asleep before arriving in town, only to wake up to discover his friends were nowhere to be seen.

"I can ask around about a job," she said. "Can you come back tomorrow?"

"I don't have anything else going on."

She pointed under the table. "What's with all the packages?"

"Do you always ask your customers so many questions?" Dusty asked, smiling at her for the first time.

"Well now, I knew you had a smile in there somewhere."

His face started to turn red. "I was just out buying some clothes. My luggage has gone missing along with my friends."

Suddenly, two people entered the diner and Cindy got up from the table.

"Come back about this same time tomorrow and I'll let you know what I find out about a job," she told him.

"I'll be here."

"I'll be expecting you then." She turned to walk away, then looked back. "And by the way, the answer is yes."

"Pardon?"

"You asked if I was single." Her next smile grabbed his heartstrings and wouldn't let go.

As Dusty got up to leave, he looked out the window. The man who had been across the street had already gone. He hadn't looked like one of the Grub's thugs. This man had been fat unlike the heavily muscled men the Grub hired.

Now that he thought about it, he'd looked more like an accountant. Albeit an unemployed accountant.

CHAPTER
FOURTEEN

BACK IN HIS ROOM AT the hotel, Dusty unpacked his purchases and placed most of them in the chest of drawers that the television rested on.

He spied a business card with the hotel name and phone number on it... probably for guests on extended stays who wanted to give the number to friends or family. He took it.

Dusty hung his dress clothes up in the closet, then sat at the small table by the window and pulled out the page with the wedding announcements and started reading it over again, this time more thoroughly than he had when looking over Tom's shoulder earlier.

He saw the announcement Tom had brought to his attention and kept reading.

No other announcements caught his eye, leaving him at a loss.

Suddenly, an idea occurred to him. He could walk back to Duggan Printing and look around that area a bit. Couldn't hurt! Plus, that whole wedding had been suspicious to him, with everyone clearing out so quickly.

Dusty headed off with his map in hand, and before he knew it he was back at Duggan Printing. Charlie's car was still parked on the street and there was a warehouse nearby, alongside a small house.

He walked up to the white wooden fence, which was in good shape. The grass was neatly cut, too, but there was no car in the driveway.

Dusty opened the gate and walked up to the house, climbing the three steps up onto the porch. He rang the doorbell and waited, but thoro wac no cound of movement inside. He knocked loudly on the door and waited a few more minutes.

Obviously no one was home.

He leaned over and peered through the picture window, cupping his hand to cut down on the reflection. The room seemed to be empty.

Though everything was well looked after, the house did not appear to be occupied. So he left and closed the gate behind him as he did so.

Scratching his head, he headed back to the hotel.

On the walk back, he had a new idea to help find out who owned the empty house. He decided that the public library would be the place to look. At least, he hoped there was a public library. Every small town had one, right?

Dusty soon arrived at the hotel, just in time for supper. He headed to the dining room and feasted on a sumptuous meal of roast duck with baby potatoes and fresh green beans. For desert he enjoyed a blackberry milkshake.

Then he headed to his room for the rest of the evening and watched television since there was nothing else to do.

• • •

The next morning, after a leisurely breakfast, Dusty headed to the front counter.

Wendy smiled at him. "How's the investigating going?"

"It's pretty boring right now." He then told her of his plans to visit the library. "That is, if you have one in town."

"You're right, that doesn't sound very exciting," she said with a big grin. "But when the guys with guns show up, you'll let me know, right?" She laughed when she saw the look of alarm on Dusty's face. "I'm just pulling your leg, Dusty. I love those exciting parts in books, but I'd rather avoid guns in real life if I can."

She pulled out a map of the town and slid it over to him, showing him where the library was located. She even pointed out the best route to get there.

Fifteen minutes later, Dusty strolled into the small public library. Despite being tiny, it had quite a few shelves lined with books, more than he had expected. He browsed for a while, curious as to what types of books he would find. He was happy to see they had some of his favorite authors in stock.

"Is there something I can help you with?"

Dusty turned around and came face to face with a woman in her mid-fifties. She had her hair up and a pair of glasses perched on her nose. A chain attached to the arms of her glasses went around her neck to prevent the glasses crashing to the floor if they ever fell off her nose.

She was the quintessential librarian.

"Yes," Dusty replied. "I came across a house today that looks like it hasn't been lived in for months. I wondered if the owners might be willing to sell. Do you know how I could find out who owns it?"

"Well, we don't have those kinds of records here. But if you go to the county office, I'm sure they can help." She gave him directions.

A short while later Dusty found the place. He opened the glass door and walked in. A few people waited in chairs against the wall, and one fellow was being helped at the counter.

Right in front of him was a stand that said *Take a number and have a seat.* He helped himself to a number, then found an empty seat and sat down to wait as the sign had instructed.

"Number 15," the woman behind the counter called out.

Dusty looked at his number. It read 20. So he was in for a bit of a wait.

He started thinking of Cindy. They'd only met the day before, but she had been so open and friendly that it already felt like he'd known her for months. Then there had been the way his heart leapt in his chest when she smiled at him...

"Number 20!"

Dusty snapped out of his thoughts, jumped up, and went up to the counter.

"I hope I'm in the right place," Dusty began. "I'm trying to locate the owner of a deserted house. They told me at the library that I might find the information here."

"This is certainly the right place, young man. Do you have the address?" The woman wore her hair in a steel grey bun and had a stern expression on her face that he envisioned an all-girls school headmistress would be proud of.

Dusty had to hand it to her, though; she knew right where to find the information he needed. Once she had the address, she pulled a file from the nearby filing cabinet.

"It says here that the house is owned by Mrs. Wilcox," she said, reading from the file.

"Does it give any contact information?"

"I can only give you a phone number."

She proceeded to read it aloud, but only after giving Dusty a pen and paper so he could write it down.

On his way to the diner afterward, Dusty passed by the police station and decided to pop in to see if Sergeant Squid Larsen was in a better frame of mind.

As Dusty pushed through the doors, he saw Larsen behind the main desk.

The man looked up and waved Dusty over. "I must apologize for my rude behavior yesterday," he said, leaning close and keeping his voice low so no one else would hear.

"Hey, no problem. If the guys at work called me Squid, I'd be in a foul mood too. How did you get that nickname anyway?"

The sergeant grimaced. "It was in training camp... when I asked the guys about it, they said I just looked like a squid. It never made any sense to me."

"I've seen pictures of squid for a report I did in high school. Trust me, you don't look anything like one."

"Thanks. I appreciate it. Now, what can I help you with?"

"I was hoping we could fill out that missing persons report."

"Sure. Let me grab the forms."

Dusty gave Larsen all the information he needed about Charlie and Tina. Then he added, "I want to report my luggage missing as well."

"Lost luggage is a matter for the airlines who lost it."

"I can't file a claim with any airline. I drove here."

"I see. Well, how did it go missing?" After hearing the story, the sergeant frowned. "Maybe your friends took it."

Dusty shook my head. "There's no way. Whoever took Charlie and Tina took my luggage—and when you find my friends, I want my luggage back."

Larsen nodded. "Makes sense." He added it to the report.

After the police station, Dusty headed back to the hotel. He wanted to call the phone number he'd gotten at the county office and find out who owned that abandoned house.

Back in his hotel room, he sat on the edge of the bed and held the paper on which he'd written the phone number. After a moment, he dialed.

The phone rang twice.

"Hello?" a women's voice said.

Dusty identified himself. "I don't know if this will make any sense..." He proceeded to tell her about the wedding, his friends' disappearance, the sinister-looking man at the wedding, and the empty house near the warehouse where the wedding had taken place.

There was silence on the other end of the line and Dusty started to think the woman had hung up. He was about to hang up as well when he heard the woman's voice.

"I think we should meet, Mr. Dusty Burns. When are you free?"

Dusty wasn't sure what to say. He was free right away, but he wanted to talk to Cindy first.

"I'm not sure right now, to be honest," he said.

"Call me when you know you'll be available, young man. By the way, my name is Ruth Wilcox. So you'll know who you're speaking to next time you call."

"I'll do that, and thank you, Mrs. Wilcox."

"Please call me Ruth.

Dusty heard a hint of laughter in her voice. So she liked to laugh...

He ended the call, found a pen in the bedside table drawer, and wrote *Mrs. Ruth Wilcox (Ruth)* above the phone number. He then folded the piece of paper and slipped it into his pocket.

Looking at the clock, he realized that it was time to go back to the diner and meet Cindy.

CHAPTER
FIFTEEN

AFTER DUSTY LEFT, SERGEANT LARSEN stared thoughtfully at the missing persons report. He hesitated on filing it just yet. For some reason, he had a feeling that Dusty Burns might just be playing a prank. Maybe the guys at the station had put him up to it, but for the life of him he couldn't see the humor in it.

He decided to hold on to it for the time being and see what unfolded. So he placed it on the desk.

Corporal Barbara Dansbury came around the corner from the hallway and walked over to the desk. "Ready to relieve you for lunch, sir."

"What? Oh, okay."

Still deep in thought, Larsen grabbed his lunch and headed to the cafeteria to eat. Barbara settled in the recently vacated chair and prepared to help anyone who came in.

A half-hour later, Larsen returned from lunch and caught Barbara reading a magazine. He had warned her not to read at the front desk.

"You are relieved, Corporal!" he said loudly.

Barbara jumped in her seat and the sergeant smiled. For some reason, it always amused him to catch Barbara doing something she shouldn't. She always had so much energy!

"I filed your report for you, sir," she said cheerfully as if trying to make up for her bad behavior.

He just stared at her. "What report?"

"The report you left lying on the desk." Her voice lost some of its enthusiasm.

Larsen felt a moment of anger but let it pass before speaking. "Oh yes, of course. Thank you."

So now it was filed and police headquarters would see a copy of it. He sure hoped it wasn't some elaborate hoax.

CHAPTER
SIXTEEN

WHEN DUSTY ENTERED THE DINER, Cindy was with another customer so he found a place at the front counter to sit and wait.

A few minutes later, she appeared in front of him smiling. "Coffee again today, Dusty?"

"Please."

"I'll get it right away. And when I come back, I've got some good news for you."

As Dusty sat waiting for his coffee, he stared absently at the door. Suddenly, it opened and the sinister-looking man from the wedding stepped inside.

Their eyes locked from across the room. Then the man turned around and quickly left.

Dusty ran towards the door, but tripped as someone sitting at the front counter stuck their leg out. Dusty crashed to the floor, stunned as his head hit the ground. He was dimly aware of someone stepping over him and the front door opening and closing.

Next thing he knew, Cindy was at his side.

"Dusty, are you okay? I saw you fall just as I was coming back to tell you the news."

Dusty sat up and within a moment his head started to clear. He soon felt well enough to stand up and get back onto his stool. His coffee was waiting for him on the counter and he took a sip. Cindy hovered by him the whole time.

"Did you see the sinister-looking man who just came in here?" Dusty asked. "He seemed a bit... elderly."

"I don't think he's elderly, not by the way he moves. But yes, I did see him. Why?"

"Do you know who he is?"

"Well, he comes in here all the time. Most days for supper. People call him Crackers—at least that's the name I've heard some call him. But that's about all I know about him. Why? Is it important?"

"I don't know. I just think he knows something about my missing friends."

"Really? I always felt there was something evil about that man."

"And I think the man sitting further down the counter tripped me as he got up and left. Do you know him too?"

"He's in pretty regularly, but I don't know his name. Sometimes he sits with Crackers. They always pay cash. I'll ask the other girl who works here and see if she's heard his name. If you give me a number where you can be reached, I'll call you if I find anything out."

She handed him a pen.

That sounded promising, so Dusty fished out the business card for the hotel he'd found in his room and wrote the phone number on a napkin.

"Let's get you into a booth so I can sit and talk to you in private for a minute," Cindy said, placing the napkin in her pocket.

They moved further back into the diner, Cindy carrying the coffee. A moment later he was seated.

"So I can't promise you a job," she said, sliding his coffee over to him. "But my father owns a warehouse and has been looking for a good forklift driver. I've set up an appointment for you to see him this afternoon at three o'clock. Does that work for you?"

"Sure does," Dusty said. "It's not like I've got a lot to do right now."

"I thought you'd say that. That's why I went ahead and made the appointment for you. It could have taken days trying to nail down a time that worked for my dad if I had to check your schedule first. It just so happens that he's free this afternoon."

"I'm glad you did. Three o'clock works just fine."

"You'll have to come by soon and let me know how it went."

"You can count on it. But won't you hear it from your dad tonight?"

"No," she said. "I don't see my dad every day."

"You don't live at home?"

Cindy laughed. "Course not, silly. I moved out on my own when I was twenty."

Dusty looked into her eyes and liked what he saw.

"I have to get back to my other customers now," she added. "But here's the address for my dad's shop. I'll see you later."

It came out sounding like a question, and since she didn't move for a few moments he decided she must be waiting for an answer.

"Yes, I'll see you soon," he said.

• • •

At a quarter to three, he had nearly walked all the way to the address Cindy had given him when he spotted a house across the street that looked familiar. Then he realized it was the same house he'd been to previously, the one owned by Mrs. Wilcox.

He found the warehouse he was looking for two buildings down and on the opposite side of the street. Parked a block up the road was Charlie's abandoned car, looking forlorn.

A man was waiting for Dusty when he stepped into the warehouse.

"You must be Dusty!" the man bellowed as he shook the young man's hand. "I'm Cindy's dad, Tony Lambert."

He was tall with a barrel chest, easy smile, and twinkling blue eyes. Dusty liked him immediately.

"Come into my office," he said as they walked together. "My daughter tells me you're looking for a job."

"Yes, sir! She said you might be able to use a good forklift driver."

"I sure could. Did you bring your certification?"

Dusty pulled out his wallet, removed the certification card, and handed it over. Cindy's father looked at it carefully, then handed it back. Dusty placed it back in his wallet.

"How long has it been since you've driven a forklift, son?"

"Four years, near as I recall. But my certification is up to date. I renewed it last year."

"Then let's go find a forklift and you can show me what you've got."

"I'd love to, sir."

They found a forklift nearby and Dusty jumped in. It was electric and Dusty felt right at home; this is what he was used to driving. He started the motor and drove it to a pallet that Cindy's dad pointed to. Dusty eased up to it, and slid the two forks under the pallet.

As soon as he lifted the pallet, he tilted the forks back a bit so the pallet was stable and wouldn't slide off the front. It was important to properly balance the load, since everything on the pallet had been shrink-wrapped right to it.

Once stabilized, Dusty lowered the pallet almost to the ground and drove it to where Cindy's father indicated. Once there he raised the forks up, moved the pallet up to the correct shelf, and lowered the pallet until it touched. Then he tilted the forks forward until the pallet was level before putting the forklift into reverse and sliding the forks out without them scraping.

Dusty was careful and efficient as he moved and stacked a few more pallets. From the man's expression, Dusty could tell that Cindy's father liked what he saw.

When Tony gestured that he'd seen enough, Dusty shut down the forklift and jumped out.

"You've got the job, son. You're very good."

"Thank you, sir!"

"Call me Tony."

They went into Tony's office, where he had some forms for Dusty to full out to make the job official.

"So what brought you to our fair town, Dusty?" Tony asked.

Even though the two had just met, Dusty liked him. He had an open face, plus he was related to Cindy, who Dusty was really starting to like.

He proceeded to tell the whole story, or at least most of it.

"I don't know any of these people you've just described, but I wish you the best of luck in finding them," Tony said.

"There's a house across the street about a half block back that way," Dusty said, pointing behind him. "Have you ever seen anyone coming or going there?"

"I havon't, but some of my workers may have. You'll meet them here tomorrow. They'd have a view of the house from where they take their breaks."

CHAPTER
SEVENTEEN

INSPECTOR BAXTER STOOD OUTSIDE SUPERINTENDENT Sanderson's closed office door. He had come to give the superintendent an update on the bank robbery. He composed his thoughts, knocked on the door, and when he heard a reply he entered.

Sanderson sat behind his desk, leaning back in his chair while talking on the telephone, one had tapping the desktop. He stopped tapping long enough to beckon Baxter in and indicate for him to sit.

Baxter had never really examined the superintendent's office and he did so now. Filing cabinets on the left side and a water cooler and credenza on the opposite wall. The credenza sat under a large window which looked out over the city of Regina's parade grounds, currently sitting empty.

Behind Sanderson were two flags crossed over each other—one of Saskatchewan and one of Canada. There was a closed door in the corner which Baxter knew held a sink and toilet.

Sanderson hung up the phone. "Well, Baxter, any new leads yet on the bank heist out of Trimble, Saskatchewan?" He seemed to catch himself. "I really need to get my brain up to speed. I don't need to say 'Saskatchewan' every time... I'm not in Ontario anymore..."

"Nothing new, sir. No clues have turned up. But we've broadened the net to include the whole surrounding area. Sadly, no people of interest have shown up on our radar and none of the money has been spent. We found the getaway car, and based on where we found it, we've been checking towns along the Saskatoon-Moose Jaw corridor, but no luck so far."

"I've been sitting here pondering the names the bank robbers used. Have you found any common thread among them?" the superintendent asked.

"Hmm. Well, as you know from the report I submitted after interviewing eye witnesses, we have the Hulk, a comic book character. Peter Pan, a children's book character. Dopey, from Snow White and the Seven Dwarves. And finally Sherlock Holmes. Everyone who was in the bank that day points to Sherlock as being the leader. Those names all come from literature... that is, if you consider a comic book literature." Baxter grinned. "I know some who would happily argue that case. Anyway, each of these characters has been in the movies. Also they all loved someone they weren't supposed to."

"They did? Who did the Hulk love?" the superintendent asked.

"General Ross's daughter, Betty."

"Okay. I know Peter Pan loved Wendy. Dopey, I think, loved Snow White... but I don't recall Sherlock Holmes ever being in love with anyone."

"Some would say that he was secretly in love with Irene Adler," Baxter suggested.

"Poppycock! I've read all the Sherlock Holmes books and, yes, she was the only one to beat him. But there was no sign of Sherlock loving anyone. So that settles that."

"Sir?"

"That trail obviously doesn't lead anywhere. It's quite clear that Sherlock wasn't in love with anyone. That was all fabricated for the movies. The movies these days seem to need romance."

"I see, sir."

"How are all the bank hostages doing now?"

Baxter hesitated for a moment before answering. "They're all doing fine, sir."

"And the senior citizen who reported the robbery? Is he holding up well?"

"From what I've been told, he's doing well and was amazingly unhurt in the affair."

"Didn't he carry one of the bags of money out to the robbers' car? Any chance he's tied up with the robbers?"

"I highly doubt it, sir. Otherwise why would he have rushed to call the police so quickly?"

"Hmm," Sanderson mused. "That does seem aboveboard. But don't let that cloud your judgement, Baxter. If he's guilty, we must discover it."

"Of course, sir."

"What other news do we have?"

"Well, sir, apart from the bank robbery, we have a report of a stolen bicycle from Outlook... and a missing persons report from Duggan."

"Check out this missing persons report. I have a feeling about that one. What do you know about it?"

Baxter pulled out his notebook and read from it. "Seems a certain Dusty Burns arrived in Duggan with two friends, Charlie Simmons and Tina Adams. Dusty was asleep in the back seat when they arrived. When he awoke, his friends and all the luggage were gone. There's been no sign of them since."

"Who do we have in that area?"

"Ted Larsen in Duggan." Baxter smiled to himself. "But he's known as Squid Larsen in those parts."

"Squid Larsen? What kind of name is that?"

"Apparently he received it while in cadet training. I don't know how he got it, though."

"That's quite the nickname. Sure, it has a nice ring to it, but it's not a name I'd use. I wonder why he keeps it..."

Baxter shrugged helplessly.

"I want you to go to Duggan and personally oversee this," Sanderson said. "We have to keep looking. Five million dollars. It's been a while since a bank was robbed for that kind of money. For all we know the robbers aren't even in province anymore. They could be in British Columbia or Ontario by now, laying low in a big city."

"I have a hunch, sir, that they're laying low right here in Saskatchewan and it'll just be a matter of time before we find them or the money. We just need a break of some kind."

CHAPTER
EIGHTEEN

DUSTY LEFT THE WAREHOUSE HAPPY to have a job where he could start paying for his hotel stay, and hopefully save up to pay back the Grub.

On his way back into town, he noticed that it was getting close to supper time. Instead of returning to the diner to give Cindy the good news, he switched direction and turned east towards the hotel and a bite to eat. His head was starting to ache a bit after the fall at the diner and he was eager to get back, eat, and rest for the evening.

The evening meal was simple but delicious. Sloppy joes with a garden salad and homemade blueberry milkshake. Dusty was very full when he walked slowly back to his room.

When he opened his door, he couldn't believe what he saw. His room had been tossed. His clothes and personal items lay all over the floor and all the drawers in the dresser had been pulled out and left haphazardly on the carpet. The lamp on the side table had fallen onto its side, the bulb broken. The bed had also been stripped.

Dusty turned and stumbled back to the front desk. He felt shocked, then angry, and then violated.

"You don't look too good," Tom told him. "Was it something you ate?"

Dusty shook his head. "My room's been broken into," he managed to croak. His voice box was a bit constricted from all the emotions flowing through him.

Tom immediately got on a radio and called someone. Then he hustled around the counter and practically ran towards Dusty's room. With his full stomach, it was all Dusty could do to keep up.

Tom inserted his master key into the lock and charged into the room. By the time Dusty entered, Tom was just standing in the middle of the room in shock.

"Whoever did this is long gone," Tom murmured.

The top mattress was lying half on the bed, half on the floor, so Dusty moved towards it to straighten it.

"Don't touch anything!" Tom exclaimed. "The police will be here shortly. They wouldn't want anything touched or moved. They'll want to see it just the way it is."

They left the room together and went back to the reception area to wait for the police to arrive.

When the police came, Dusty recognized one of the officers. If it wasn't his good ol' pal Ted "Squid" Larsen! And there was a second officer with him.

The pair took a look in the room, then taped it off with a police line.

"Our crime scene technician will be here tomorrow to dust for prints," Larsen explained. "He doesn't live right in Duggan. He services a few towns around this area."

"So I can't access my room for the night?" Dusty asked.

"Don't worry about that," Tom said. "We have other rooms available. We'll put you up in one of those until this is cleared up. We'll provide toothbrush, toothpaste, and all your other toiletries. I'll go arrange that right now." He walked off.

"Once our technician does his thing, you can go back into your room," Larsen assured him. "Have you noticed anything missing?"

"Are you kidding? I'd have to clean up the room to tell that."

"Right, right. Okay, I'll come back tomorrow after the technician is finished and see if you can tell if anything is missing."

"Sure," Dusty said. "And when will you be looking into my missing persons report?"

"Headquarters is sending a man down to head that up."

"Any idea when he might show up?"

"He could arrive any day. But I'd imagine it will be soon. I'll call the hotel when he arrives. That is, if he wants to talk to you."

"Thanks, Squid."

The sergeant glared at him and then stalked away.

Dusty called after him, "Sorry, I meant Sergeant Larsen!" But he got no response.

CHAPTER
NINETEEN

"YOU DID *WHAT*?" CRACKERS YELLED. His face was purple with rage.

Jackson Tate and Peter Grimsby stood in front of him, looking ashamed. Crackers sat behind his desk in the spartan office. Vi stood off to the side, her arms folded across her chest, looking bored with the whole ordeal.

There was nothing else in the room except Crackers's desk and the chair he sat in.

"We trashed that fellow's hotel room," Jackson said. "You know... to scare him a bit so he'll stop poking around."

"First you grab his two buddies, and now this! Pretty soon you'll have the cops crawling down our necks," Crackers replied. "At least one of you had the foresight to clear out the wedding crowd when their friend came poking around. I sort of expect these hare-brained behaviors from Grimsby, but I expect more from you, Jackson."

Jackson bowed his head. "Sorry, boss."

"The two people we grabbed weren't really our fault, boss," Grimsby said. "The man and the lady came in the door just as we were wheeling in the last bunch of money in an old laundry cart. We had the cart covered so they couldn't see in, and then... well, I'm not sure how it happened. The cart hit something, maybe the corner of the wall, and tipped. The money fell out. Those two just stood and stared, their eyes as big as saucers. I recognized them as out-of-towners so I had to grab them. They could have hit the road otherwise and called the cops. They can't rat us out. Not now."

"You already told mo this, Grimsby. Remember?" Crackers turned to Vi. "But now we have to keep returning to that building to take care of them. Someone will see us going in and out of there and think we're open for business. They'll bring us something they need printed. And they'll get mighty curious when we can't print anything for them."

"Don't look at me!" Vi said. "I'm not babysitting those two. Jackson and Grimsby made this mess. They can clean it up."

Crackers shifted his attention back to Grimsby and Jackson. "So what brilliant plan do you guys have so that people won't traipse in and out of Duggan Printing every single day?"

"We have them locked in a back room," said Jackson. "One that conveniently has a bathroom with a sink and shower. They have their luggage and we gave them enough food to last a week. They can get water from the sink, boss."

Jackson frowned. "I don't get why a printing company would have an office with a full bathroom and shower…"

Crackers looked at the big man disdainfully. "It wasn't always a printing company."

"So what was it before?" Jackson asked.

"I seem to recall the realtor telling me it used to be a hospital, and then an orphanage a long time ago. More recently, someone used it as a doctor's office. I think it sat empty for years before I bought it. That's why I got it for a song."

"At least we have them locked up now," Grimsby pointed out. "And they can't go to the police with what they know."

Crackers just stared at him. "Listen. Those two may still go the cops if we let them go. And even with no evidence, the police will watch us. We can't have that. We just can't."

"So what are we going to do?" Grimsby asked.

"Okay, this is contrary to what I said a minute ago, but it just occurred to me that we can't leave them unsupervised," Vi piped up. "We have to check on them periodically. We can bring them fresh sheets and towels so they don't know what we're really doing. But in reality we'll surreptitiously make sure they aren't digging a hole through the wall."

Jackson looked unhappy about this suggestion. "What? Are we running a hotel here now?"

"I say shoot them," Grimsby said.

"You always want to shoot someone!" Crackers yelled. "It's not healthy. Okay, this is what we're going to do: we'll keep an eye on those two, but stay away from that fellow you've been following. What did you say his name was?"

"The girl at the diner called him Dusty," Grimsby said.

"Right, stay away from Dusty. I hear he's got the police involved and that's too hot for us."

Grimsby put his hands on his hips. "But he might have seen us the night they arrived in town."

"He was sleeping," Jackson replied. "There's no way he saw us."

"How do you know he wasn't faking?"

"Boys, boys," Crackers broke in. "You're starting to sound like a couple of old women."

"At least the lady has shut up now that she has her luggage," Grimsby said.

Jackson shook his head. "Are you kidding? Sure, she has her luggage, but she's always needing to wash her clothes. The other day she asked me to wash her socks for her. Can you believe that?"

CHAPTER
TWENTY

NOW THAT DUSTY HAD A job, he woke up early and thought he was still back in his original room—that is, until he got up and couldn't find any clothes in the dresser. He looked at his watch and saw that it was five o'clock in the morning. Then he remembered he was in a temporary room assignment until the police were finished with the crime scene.

So he dressed in his clothes from the night before and went out to see if the crime scene technician had come yet. When he found the room still taped off, he went for breakfast.

After he finished a hearty meal of eggs and bacon, he headed back to his original room and found the door open and the tape removed. He started to walk inside.

"Whoa there!" a voice said. A man's head poked out from the bedroom. "You can't come in here. What are you doing here anyway?"

"I live here," Dusty replied. "And I need fresh clothes so I can go to work and not stink."

The crime scene technician was wearing slacks and a standard police jacket. He wore surgical gloves.

"I still can't let you in," the man said. "You might contaminate the area."

Dusty saw that his clothes were no longer on the floor and that the dresser drawers had been put back in place. His clothes were probably back in the dresser.

"Could you at least open my dresser drawers and grab me a fresh set of clothes?" Dusty said. "Then I'll be out of your hair for the rest of the day."

The technician looked at him for a long moment, then nodded. He strode over to the chest of drawers and pulled out a clean pair of jeans, socks, and a long-sleeved shirt.

"It's a bit nippy out," the man said.

Dusty noticed his gloved hand hesitate over the underwear in the bottom drawer.

"It's brand new," Dusty told him. "Never been worn."

So the technician picked up a pair with his index finger and thumb and held it away from himself. He walked up to Dusty and piled the clothes in his arms with the underwear on top.

"So why did the police send you here?" Dusty asked. "I thought that only happens when there's a death involved."

"Normally that's true. But this is a small community and the owners of the hotel are well-respected. Anyway, I didn't ask why when I got the call to come. I just came."

"Fair enough. Well, I'll leave you to it then." Dusty backed out of the room and headed to the other room to shower and change into his fresh clothes.

• • •

When Dusty walked into the warehouse a couple of hours later, he looked for Tony but didn't see him. While he was searching, a man he didn't know approached. The name on his tag was *Jerry Berilo*, and smaller letters underneath added the detail that he was the foreman.

Jerry didn't look too happy to see him.

"You must be Dusty," he snarled. "Don't think that you'll get any special treatment just because the boss hired you!" He turned and stalked away, but not before muttering, "It's my job to hire new staff! I'll get rid of this guy soon enough. Just you wait and see…"

Dusty stood rooted to the spot, floored by the foreman's reception and unsure what to do next.

"Well, don't just stand there," Jerry bellowed. "I have to show you around today. Apparently the boss can't be bothered to do this even though he's the one who hired you…"

He took off at a fast pace, still muttering to himself. Dusty hurried to catch up.

Jerry showed him the warehouse. Stacks and stacks of merchandise filled the giant room with aisles between the rows. Wooden pallets lay in the aisles, some with partial loads placed on them and others with nothing on them at all.

Jerry was cantankerous and rude the whole time, yet Dusty still got a good sense of the layout. What he couldn't figure out was why Jerry was being such a pain in the butt. Was he always like that or was he just having an abnormally bad day? Dusty didn't want to ask, so he kept his mouth shut and followed Jerry around.

"You see those flat wooden pallets on the floor?" Jerry asked sarcastically.

"Sure, I see them."

"When they have merchandise stacked on them and wrapped in plastic, they're ready for you bring to the loading bay."

No kidding, dum-dum, Dusty thought.

"We have store merchandise, car and farm machinery parts, agricultural fertilizer, tractor parts, planting seed, grass seed, spades, hoes… you name it."

Dusty saw all that and much more. He observed bulk boxes with store names on them, and bulk boxes of labelled paper towels, cereal, and kitchen utensils. There was just so much to store in this medium-sized warehouse. Prior to this, Dusty had always worked in relatively small warehouses.

"What's in the crates with store names printed on them?" Dusty asked.

"What do you think, mouse traps? Clothes, boy! There's clothes in there. What are you, dumb? We service all the stores around this area. Not just in Duggan. For a lot of the small stores, we are their storeroom. Most of them are too small to keep so much inventory on hand."

He spoke in a very condescending tone and glared at Dusty throughout his speech.

It seemed to Dusty that if Jerry wasn't pleased with anything in the warehouse, he'd view it somehow as Dusty's fault.

Jerry broke Dusty's train of thought by rambling on. "We even have a famous musician whose home is close by. He stores all his equipment and instruments here. In fact, he has a 1970 Martin D35 acoustic guitar stored here with the rest of his things!"

If that was supposed to mean anything to Dusty, it didn't. He just looked blankly at Jerry.

"You really are dumb, boy! The Martin D35 has a beautiful tone! The playability is amazing and the sound gets better over time. Do you know what that means?" He waited for Dusty to respond. When no response came, he bellowed, "It means it's high-quality! This guitar is much in demand and it's sought-after by a lot of musicians even today."

Dusty didn't know what to say. He found it hard to get excited about a guitar he'd never heard of before.

Jerry threw up his arms in exasperation. "You've seen enough of this area. Let's go find your forklift so you can get started. Do you think you can handle that?"

What a jerk!

"Yeah, I can handle it."

Jerry didn't reply; he simply turned around and walked back to the other side of the warehouse and the office area.

Dusty ran to keep up. He felt like a little boy.

En route they converged with a red-haired young man by the forklift Dusty was to drive. The redhead looked relaxed in jeans, a T-shirt, and comfortable-looking shoes.

"This is Red," Jerry barked. "He's the shipper receiver and will show you what he needs to get done. If you have questions, don't bother me. Ask him!" He jerked his thumb in Red's direction as if to emphasize that point. "And if you screw up in any way, I'll make your life miserable."

Jerry turned and headed towards his office.

CHAPTER
TWENTY-ONE

AFTER JERRY WENT INTO HIS office, Red stuck out his hand. Dusty shook it.

"Hi, welcome aboard! You're the new forklift operator, right?"

"Yeah, I am." Dusty kept his eyes on Jerry sitting down in his office. "What's up with him? Is he always like this?"

"Oh, don't worry about Jerry! He just hates you because the owner hired you. To be honest, he doesn't really like anyone. I guess some guys just enjoy being miserable."

"Does everyone know that I was hired by the boss and not Jerry?"

"There aren't that many of us here, so yeah, pretty much."

While Dusty talked to Red, he checked out the forklift. It wasn't the same machine he had driven as part of his job interview and he wanted to make sure it was safe. He didn't trust that Jerry had inspected it thoroughly.

He checked the forks for any damage, cracks, or bends in the metal. The forks needed to be perfectly straight or the strength of the forks would be compromised. It was the forks that carried the whole weight of the load. Then he checked the chain which hoisted the forks into the air; it looked well oiled. There was no sign of rust, a good sign that the machine was well cared for. He did a walk around the forklift and didn't see any damage to the body.

"What do you need me to do now?" Dusty asked.

"Right now it's time for a coffee break. Follow me."

Three minutes later they were seated in the break room at a round table that had room for four. Red drank coffee and Dusty had a cup of water.

Dusty took a sip. "How long have you worked here?"

"Three years."

"What did you do before?"

"A little of this and that. I tried manual labor, but it wasn't for me. Then I worked retail for a while."

"So how'd you end up here?"

"Got tired of working weekends in retail. Here it's Monday to Friday with weekends off."

"What if a store needs merchandise on a Saturday?" Dusty asked. "Say they're out of whatever the customer needs? Doesn't the warehouse need to be open so they can get the merchandise out to the store if need be?"

"The store just tells the customer they can't get it until Monday."

"I guess."

Red looked him over carefully. "So I've never seen you around town before. Are you new here?

"Well, yeah, I came here with two friends of mine."

"You moved to Duggan?"

"Not really." Then he told Red what had brought him to town, and that his friends had gone missing.

"I'm really sorry to hear about that. Let me know if I can help in any way."

By this time, Red had finished his coffee. He got up. "Time to head back to work."

Dusty got up and emptied what was left of his cup of water into the sink before following Red out of the break room.

For the next couple of hours, Dusty drove the forklift. He picked up the pallets that were loaded and wrapped in plastic and drove them to the loading bay. When two trucks showed up, he loaded the pallets into the truck that Red indicated.

And so ended Dusty's first shift.

After the forklift had been parked for the day, he and Red left together.

When they got outside Dusty pointed to the building down the street. "Do you ever see anyone going in or out of that house there?" he asked. Then he pointed to the left. "Or how about to that printing business there?"

Red scratched his chin. "Never for the house. But sometimes... these are rare occasions, mind you, times when we have a late shipment and I don't get out of here until 5:00 or 6:00... well, then I think I've seen people going in or coming out of Duggan Printing. But I never paid much attention, you know?"

"Have you recognized anyone you knew around Duggan Printing?"

"Not that I recall. But if I remember anything, I'll let you know."

"I'd appreciate that. See you tomorrow then."

Red waved and headed off. Dusty went off in the other direction, towards the diner to see Cindy.

The restaurant was mostly empty. The lunch crowd had gone and it was too early yet for the supper crowd. One lone man sat at the counter and Cindy was just refilling his cup when Dusty walked through the door.

Cindy turned, and when she saw Dusty her face lit up in a big, hundred-watt smile. She set the coffee pot on the back counter behind her, then hurried around and out into the open, her eyes bright and shining.

"So did you get the job?" she asked.

"I did! I just got off my first shift."

Cindy squealed and threw her arms around him, hugging him tightly. Then she stepped back as if she had crossed a line. "I'm sorry. That was a bit forward of me."

Dusty was a bit taken back by her move, but he liked it. "Don't feel bad. You can throw your arms around me anytime."

She flashed another smile. "Let's find you a table and sit down. I want to hear all about it."

Once Dusty was seated and Cindy had gotten him a cup of coffee, she plopped into the seat. He told her about the interview with her dad and how well it had gone.

"He was very nice," he said. "The job today, though, was only okay. It was overshadowed by the foreman. He was a real jerk!"

"What do you mean? What did he do?"

"He was rude and obnoxious and threatened to make my life miserable if I screw up."

"Oh, don't mind Jerry. His bark is much worse than his bite."

Dusty took a sip from his coffee. "You sound like you know him."

"He's worked for my dad for years, so I'd see him at company picnics growing up. Dad even had him over to the house from time to time." Cindy suddenly snapped her fingers. "I talked to Veronika, the other girl who works here, yesterday after my shift. She didn't know the name of the fellow who tripped you in here. Sorry."

"All right. Thanks for asking." He paused. "So getting back to Jerry... you don't think I have anything to worry about?"

"Of course not, silly."

CHAPTER
TWENTY-TWO

DUSTY ORDERED LUNCH AT THE diner. It was fairly inexpensive and saved him the time of walking back to the motel. Plus he had a job now, so he could afford it.

He was just finishing up a hamburger and fries when Cindy came back and sat herself down in the seat across from him.

"So when are we going to sleuth together?" she asked.

Dusty snapped his fingers. "I forgot to tell you something. I went poking around the area where my friends disappeared and found a house with the yard all kept up. But when I peeked in a window, the place was bare. I was hoping someone there might have seen something that will help me locate my friends. So I tracked down the owner. Well, her phone number anyway. I called her and got the woman's first name, the county office gave me her last name. Anyway, she said I should come over so she can tell me about that house. Here, I think I still have the slip of paper in my pocket."

He dug around in all his pockets and finally pulled out the paper where he'd scrawled down the woman's name.

"Here it is. Mrs. Ruth Wilcox. And I've got her phone number… but I'll have to go back to the hotel to make the call. Or is there a phone here I can use?"

"Where is this house again?" Cindy asked.

"Same street as the warehouse your dad owns."

"That's tenth street then."

"Yes, I guess it is. I haven't memorized the street numbers yet. Just been working on knowing my way around. So… is there a phone here?"

"Not one you can use."

Dusty looked dejected.

"But there's one I can use," she said with a grin. Cindy bounced out of her seat and gently pulled the slip of paper from Dusty's fingers. "I'll be right back."

A few minutes later, she returned and slid the paper over to him. He saw there was an address now written on it.

"Is this close by?" he asked.

"About a five- to seven-minute walk, I'd say," Cindy said. "I get off work in twenty minutes. Will you wait for me? I told Ruth Wilcox we'd be coming together in thirty minutes. Hope you don't mind."

Dusty smiled. "I don't mind at all."

He had another cup of coffee and gazed out the window. He recalled the day when he'd come in and first spied that man watching him from across the street. Had the Grub's men found him? But if so, why hadn't he seen anyone since then?

These thoughts were running through his mind when suddenly he felt a hand on his shoulder.

He looked up and saw Cindy, ready to go. She had a purse slung over her shoulder and sunglasses in her hand.

"Didn't you hear me?" she asked.

"I guess not."

"You did look pretty deep in thought. Let's go. You can tell me about it on the way."

After they got out the door and started down the sidewalk, Dusty told her about the guy he had seen watching him from across the street.

"Interesting," she said. "If it's not the guys you owe money to, who could it be?"

Dusty just shrugged his shoulders.

"Oh we're here!" Cindy exclaimed as they reached a tidy house with a wooden picket fence.

They walked up to the house and climbed the three steps. They looked at each other for a moment, then Cindy inclined her head towards the house and Dusty knocked.

The door was opened almost immediately by an elderly woman with hair white as snow. She also had a big smile on her face.

"You must be the ones who called me," Mrs. Wilcox said. "Dusty and Cindy, I believe? Come in, come in."

She led them into the living room.

"Have a seat. Is there anything I can get you to drink?"

"Cold water would be nice," Cindy said.

"Oh yes, I imagine so. It's a warm day out there. You just relax and I'll be right back with two glasses of cold water."

Cindy and Dusty looked around the room. There was a hutch in the corner with some nice little figurines and some good china—at least, that's what Dusty figured if they were on display like that.

He also spotted a big Bible sitting squarely on the coffee table. He noticed Cindy looking at it too and raised his eyebrows in a question. She shook her head and gave a tiny, almost imperceptible shrug just as Mrs. Wilcox came back in the room. She carried a round silver tray with two tall glasses full of water and ice cubes.

She set the tray down. "I see you are interested in my Bible."

Dusty looked up, a bit shocked that'd he'd been noticed.

"Do you read the Bible, dear?"

"Um, no," he said. "Do you read it?"

"Yes, dear, I do. I've had that Bible since I was a young woman. It's like a cherished family member in some ways. I've written so many notes in there. It's dear to me. The Bible is a good mirror, you know."

"Some Christians I've met use the Bible to judge," Cindy replied.

"Oh dear. Yes, I've met some of those too. But you see, a mirror is to hold up and perceive what you look like in it. It's not for holding up and showing others what they look like. But enough about that for now. Let's talk about the reason you came to see me. You found a house that seems a bit suspicious to you and it was listed in my name. Is that about right?"

Dusty nodded. "Um, yes. I think it ties in somehow to the disappearance of my two friends. And I'd like to find them."

"This may be a bit of a shock to you, but I was married for years to a very unpleasant man named Craggy McBean."

Dusty looked at Cindy, but her face showed no recognition of that name.

"All his buddies called him Crackers," Mrs. Wilcox added.

"Crackers," Dusty said, turning to Cindy. "That's the name of the guy you've seen in the diner." He looked back to Mrs. Wilcox, "Wait a minute. You were married to this guy? Why is the house in your name if you're no longer married?"

"That's a very good question," she said. "The house was purchased by my ex-husband, but he likes to avoid putting his name on anything. When we were married he put everything in my name, and even now he continues to do that. I suppose I could sell that house if I wanted to and all the proceeds would be mine." Mrs. Wilcox smiled happily at the thought. "You know, I never even thought of that before."

Cindy smiled back at Mrs. Wilcox.

"Do you know where we could find Craggy McBean?" Dusty asked.

"No, dear, I don't. But he owns a lot of houses and I'll bet he lives in one of them."

"Do you have any idea how we could find all the houses he owns?"

"It's simple, dear. Just find all the houses that are listed under my name. He'll be in one of them, I'm sure."

CHAPTER
TWENTY-THREE

DUSTY HEADED TO THE DINER after work the following day to see Cindy. The place was busy. He hadn't seen it so busy since he had first started coming.

When he finally caught Cindy's eye, he worked his way towards her.

"What's going on here?" he asked above the steady murmur of chatter from the customers.

"Convention in town. It should drop off and clear out in an hour or so if you want to come back. Everyone from the convention got out late so they're having a late lunch."

"Sounds good. I'll see you later."

Dusty smiled at Cindy and got a sweet grin in return.

Next Dusty headed to the hotel. On his way to check whether the technician was finished with his original room, he heard Wendy call over from the front counter.

"I have a message for you," she said, excitedly clutching a note in her right hand. "From the police. Sergeant Larsen says there's an inspector there who'd like to speak with you about your missing friends."

Wendy looked up from the note to see that Dusty had already turned around, heading out the front door at a fast pace.

When Dusty got to the police station, he opened the glass door and went inside. The first person he saw was Larsen talking to a dark-haired man dressed in casual clothes. The newcomer was leaning over the desk with a store-bought coffee cup in his hand.

Larsen looked up when Dusty entered. The dark-haired man straightened up.

"This is the fellow who filed the report," Larsen said to the man. As Dusty got closer, the sergeant made introductions. "Dusty Burns, meet Inspector Baxter. Inspector Baxter, meet Dusty Burns."

"I'd like to talk to you about your missing friends, if that's okay by you," Inspector Baxter said. Dusty nodded and Baxter turned back to Larsen. "Is there a private room we can use to talk?"

Larsen shook his head. "It's such a small place..."

"Where can we go?" Baxter asked.

Dusty glanced back towards the door. "Well, there's the diner."

Baxter raised his eyebrows, as if indicating he needed to hear more.

"It's not usually too busy at this time of day, but there's a crowd from a convention in town having a late lunch," Dusty explained. "They should be clearing out soon."

Baxter turned to Larsen as if for confirmation. Larsen nodded his agreement.

"That sounds perfect," the inspector said. "Shall we head off then?"

They walked over together, and for a while the inspector fell back a couple paces to let Dusty lead.

"So how did you end up in this town?" Baxter asked when they were still a few blocks from the diner.

"With my buddies. You know, the two I filed the missing persons report about—"

"I know about your buddies. I read that report. I mean, what brought you here? Why did you leave wherever you lived before?"

Dusty told him about his business and the loan shark, telling the story of how he'd been unable to pay back the loan in time. As he talked, the inspector sipped happily on his coffee.

"Are you listening to anything I'm saying?" Dusty asked.

Baxter gave him a blank stare. "Now, why did your friends come with you if the loan shark was only after you?"

"They didn't want me to go alone, I guess. It's only been a few days... yet it seems like it's been weeks..."

The inspector nodded in understanding.

When they arrived, Dusty opened the door and went into the diner. Baxter dropped his now-empty cup in the garbage just outside the door and followed Dusty inside.

As soon as they took a seat, Cindy appeared to take their order. "What can I get you?"

"Hi Cindy," Dusty said. "This is Inspector Baxter. He's up from police headquarters in Regina to look into my missing friends."

"That's great!" Cindy exclaimed.

"I'll take a coffee," Baxter said. "Two cream, two sugar. A double-double is what they call it in the city."

Cindy turned to Dusty. "And for you?"

"Just a water will be fine."

After she brought the drinks, Cindy hovered by the table as though wanting to say something more.

"Young lady," said Baxter, "thanks for bringing our drinks. Now, if you don't mind, Dusty and I would like to have a private conversation."

Cindy looked imploringly at Dusty.

"It's okay, Inspector," Dusty told him. "Cindy knows all about this."

Baxter raised an eyebrow. "Really? Well then, let me ask you this, young lady: have you noticed any strangers around in the past few months? You know, seeing as you're a local."

"I saw a stranger," Dusty blurted out. "Well, okay, I wouldn't know who was a stranger here… but I saw some strange behaviour."

"Do tell."

Dusty went on to explain that he'd seen a man on the other side of the street watching him in the diner one day.

"What did the man look like?" Baxter asked sharply.

Dusty was a bit taken aback by the inspector's tone of voice, but he went ahead and shared all the details he could remember.

"What I recall is that he was fat and wore a rumpled tan trench coat," Dusty said. "He had dark hair. Oh! And he wore glasses. I remember that it was raining, and the rain was running down over them and he kept taking them off and wiping the water off the lenses, then putting them back on."

When Dusty finished, Baxter looked towards Cindy with a thoughtful expression on his face.

"I haven't seen any strangers around." Cindy smiled. "Not unless you count Dusty here."

The inspector raised his eyebrows in surprise. "You said yourself that you've only been in town a few days. How is it that you two seem to know each other so well?"

"We just hit it off," Cindy said with a smile. "Ever since the first day that Dusty came in."

"It's true," Dusty said.

"Okay. We'll be looking into what happened to your friends. But leave this to the police. I don't want you two getting in the way here."

"It's a little late for that," Dusty replied.

Inspector Baxter's face started to turn an angry red. "What? You two have already been investigating on your own?"

"All I did was look through the local paper for wedding announcements on the day Charlie and Tina went missing."

"Right. That wedding you stumbled upon where everyone dispersed in a most guilty fashion."

"Exactly. Then I went to look at the house listed in one of the announcements, but there was nothing there but an abandoned lot."

Baxter gave Dusty a very stern look. "Is that all you did?"

"No," he admitted. "I also went to the county office, where they gave me the phone number for the owner, Mrs. Ruth Wilcox."

"Dusty and I went to see her yesterday," Cindy added.

"If the house in question is owned by her, then she's a suspect. I wish you hadn't gone to see her."

"I think you'll be glad we did," Dusty said. "Because she informed us that her ex-husband, Crackers, the man we think is involved in Charlie and Tina's disappearance, puts all his properties in her name. If you look up all these properties, you'll likely find Crackers living in one of them."

"Still, it would have been better if you'd let me talk to her."

"Nothing is stopping you from doing that, sir. Why don't you talk to her today?"

Inspector Baxter stood up and placed the money for his coffee on the table. "That's a good idea. In the meantime, I don't want either of you poking your noses where they don't belong! Is that clear?"

"Crystal clear," Dusty and Cindy said in unison.

After the inspector had gone, Cindy sat down at the table with Dusty. "Wow! It really seems like we'll be in trouble if he catches us investigating. So what do we do now?"

"Something tells me we don't want to get on his bad side," Dusty replied. "I guess we just do our jobs and see what happens."

CHAPTER
TWENTY-FOUR

THE NEXT FEW DAYS WENT by quickly. Dusty worked closely with Red, and they became fast friends. Each day consisted of a busy morning with a coffee break in the middle. Then came lunch, another hour or two of work, depending on how busy they were, and they'd call it a day and go home when the work slowed down.

"So how long have you lived in Duggan?" Dusty asked one day over lunch.

"My family has lived here, at least in this area, for several generations," Red explained.

"I see. Well, what is there to do around here when one isn't working?"

"There's actually plenty to do. What have you been doing after work until now?"

"I usually go to the diner, you know?" Dusty said. "There's someone I like seeing there."

"You like Cindy? Oh, this is juicy!"

"How on earth did you know it was Cindy?"

"She's the only one I ever see when I go there. Besides Gus, who does the cooking in the back. You don't go there to see Gus, do you?"

"Of course not!"

"Now, don't be hurt. I'm just having a bit of fun with you." Red laughed. "But speaking of things to do around here, my family owns a nature preserve called Floggin's Bog."

"Floggin's bog? Your last name is Floggin?"

"It's my mother's maiden name. My maternal grandfather started the preserve back in the 40s. You should come check it out sometime. It's quite a nice place to go for a walk."

"You can't be serious!" Dusty protested. "Do you even know what a bog is? It's a smelly cesspool full of all kinds of vile, putrid odors!"

"It's a nature preserve, like I told you. Sure, there's a bog there, but it's just a small part of the whole place. There are plants, trees, birds, trails, benches to sit on and enjoy the view... you'll like it. You should invite Cindy too. Next weekend is supposed to be excellent weather. We should go together and take advantage of it. I'll bring my Labrador retriever."

"Promises, promises. I'll tell you what: I'll talk to Cindy and see what she has to say about going to a bog. By the way, if you bring your dog and I bring Cindy, won't it be like a double date?"

Red grinned. "Not likely, buddy. You and Cindy will be the only ones on a date."

Dusty laughed and clapped Red on the shoulder as they got ready to return to work.

Occasionally one or both of the order pickers at the warehouse joined them for lunch, but usually the pickers were finished and had left for the day by the time lunchtime rolled around. Still, Dusty got to talk to them occasionally and learned that one was Tim Beadle and other Warren Meechum. He also heard that their families were farmers and they usually helped out on the farm in the afternoons and evenings.

Dusty also discovered that Red's real name was Toby Lutz, but everyone just called him Red, including his family. His Labrador retriever's name was Rex... Rex Lutz.

"I think your dog's name is cooler than yours," Dusty told him as they walked around the warehouse.

"I think you're right. Don't tell him, though. It might go to his head."

After work that day, Dusty dropped by the diner. Cindy was serving other customers when he arrived, so he headed to the back to find a booth. Another man was seated in the booth next to him, with his back to Dusty.

Once Dusty settled in and got a closer look, he realized that the man was none other than Inspector Baxter.

A few minutes later, Cindy plunked down in the seat opposite him, her eyes bright and shiny. "So how is your day going?"

"Very well." He grinned. "Well, even better now."

Cindy blushed, then rested her hand on Dusty's. "I'm so happy your day gets better when you see me."

She squeezed his hand, and Dusty squeezed back. They spent a moment looking at each other without talking.

Finally, Dusty broke the silence. "Uh, Red invited me to go to Floggin's Bog. Have you ever been there?"

"Red from the warehouse?"

"Why? Do you know any other people named Red?"

Cindy smiled. "Hmm, no, can't say that I do. And no, I've never been to Floggin's Bog. I hear it has nice walking trails."

"That's what I heard too, plus plants, birds, and maybe even some wildlife. Red wants to take me out there sometime soon. Would you like to come along?"

"Oh my, you said the magic words. Yes, I'd love to go with you!"

"Right on! Uh... magic words? You mean 'would you like to come along'?"

"No, silly. 'Birds and wildlife.'"

CHAPTER
TWENTY-FIVE

DUSTY HAD AN UNEVENTFUL WEEKEND, talked to Tom and Wendy, hung out with Cindy, and enjoyed a break from work. Dusty also cleaned up his room and put his clothes back in the order he preferred, from the haphazard way the technician had thrown them in the drawers. He did not find anything missing and planned to tell Larsen that the next time he saw him.

On Monday, Dusty told Red the good news: "So I asked Cindy to go to Floggin's Bog with me and she said yes!"

"Congratulations, man! Now all that's left is for me to ask my dog, and of course pick a day to go."

Dusty burst out laughing and they both headed back to work.

At lunch, when they were finished eating, Dusty and Red stepped outside for some sunshine and fresh air.

"You know, I find it strange that Duggan Printing never has any deliveries," Dusty said. "Or customers or employees coming or going. I find that particularly odd for a printing business."

"Maybe we should check it out?"

"No need. I've tried the door numerous times and it's always locked."

"We still have fifteen minutes left of our lunch break. I say we try it."

And with that, Red started walking across the street at a fast clip.

Dusty ran to catch up. "It'll be locked like always. And besides, I get the creeps around that building."

"Aw, come on. What can it hurt?"

Within a minute they came to the door. Red tried the latch and the door opened. Dusty stood there with his mouth open in surprise.

Red stepped inside.

"W–what are you doing?" Dusty stammered.

"I just want to look around."

So Dusty followed him in, the door shutting behind them with an audible click. Dusty jumped at the sound.

"Your nerves are a bit on edge, buddy," Red said. "Calm down and just relax."

The entryway was dim and Dusty couldn't see much, but he could see enough of Red to follow him though the double swinging doors up ahead.

They walked into a large room, the same room where last time he was here Dusty had seen people dressed up for a wedding. Red headed to the back wall, the wall Crackers had disappeared behind that night. It seemed so long ago to Dusty, yet it was less than two weeks.

"Where are you going?" Dusty's voice cracked. His throat felt very dry.

"I'm looking for the restroom."

"Use the restroom back at the warehouse!"

"Not sure if I can last that long. There has to be a restroom somewhere close by. Don't worry, it'll just take a minute and we'll be gone."

As Red went off in search of the restroom, Dusty ducked behind the wall and soon found himself in the hallway once again. Red was about ten feet to Dusty's left when he stopped in front of a door.

"Ah, just what I was looking for."

Red opened the door and entered.

When Dusty got a little closer, he saw the sign on the door: *Gents*. It had the universal image of a man right below it.

Dusty continued on down the hallway, coming up to a second door. This one also had a sign: *Keep Out*. He shrugged and tried the doorknob. It was locked but loose in its frame, so Dusty gave it a solid hip check. The door popped open.

Inside, Dusty fumbled around in the dark until he found the light switch. He turned it on, bathing the small room in light. The room was filled with cloth bags. Curious, Dusty opened one and looked inside.

Money. Scores of cash.

He closed the bag and tried another. Same thing. He closed that one up and opened a third. More cash.

"What are you doing?" a voice boomed behind Dusty.

Dusty jumped and his heart almost stopped. He quickly closed the bag, then turned cautiously to find Red in the doorway, grinning from ear to ear.

When he could breathe again and his heart slowed down to a normal speed, Dusty pushed Red out into the hallway. He shut off the light and popped the door closed again with a sharp, powerful tug.

"What was in those bags?" Red asked.

"Cash. Lots and lots of cash."

Somewhere in the building, they heard a door slam. Dusty turned pale.

Red took him by the arm and propelled him down the hall into the large room by the front entrance.

"Don't worry," he whispered in Dusty's ear. "I've got you. Everything will be okay."

Dusty could hardly breathe. He had just found a huge stash of money, been scared out of his wits by Red, and now he could hear footsteps clicking on tile flooring. Someone was coming—and if they were caught, he was sure they would be killed.

Red seemed to read the expression on Dusty's face and sped up. Soon they were out through the double swinging doors into the gloom.

It felt to Dusty like his vision was fading. *I'm not going to make it...*

Before he knew it, they burst out the front door into bright sunlight. Red let go of him and quietly closed the door behind them. He took Dusty by the elbow, angled him back across the street to the warehouse, where inside they both collapsed on the floor.

CHAPTER
TWENTY-SIX

DUSTY AND RED GOT BACK to work once the adrenaline had left their bodies and they could stand again.

Dusty couldn't stop thinking about all that money. Something crooked was going on in that building and he felt quite strongly that he should tell the police about it.

Time started to drag as the shift wore on.

"I have to take a bathroom break," Dusty said after a while.

"Can't you wait? We'll be done in like ten to twenty minutes."

"I won't last that long. I'll make it quick."

"Okay, but hurry. I want to go home."

Dusty left the warehouse and walked past the offices on his way to the bathroom. As he passed Jerry's office, he heard the foreman call out to him.

"Dusty, is that you?" Jerry barked.

"Uh, yes…"

"What are you doing?"

"I'm just going to use the bathroom."

"Well, don't expect me to come hold your hand!" Jerry glared at Dusty. "We're not running a daycare here! Now, be quick about it and get back to work."

• • •

After work, Dusty made a beeline for the police station. He was out of breath by the time he arrived.

When he burst through the door, Inspector Baxter and Squid Larsen were deep in conversation at the front desk.

"Dusty! What's up? You look a little out of breath." Inspector Baxter led Dusty to a chair. "Here, take a seat. What has you all worked up?"

Dusty sat, dripping with sweat. "Money, lots of money," he said between gasps.

"Money? Where did you see this money? Calm down. Try to take some deep breaths. There now… now, start from the beginning."

As soon as Dusty's breathing slowed, he leaned forward in the chair and told them about his visit to Duggan Printing. They interrupted him just as he got to the part about finding the money bags in the locked back room.

"You closed the locked door again after you found the money?" Baxter asked.

"I sure did."

Next Dusty told them about hearing footsteps and fleeing with Red.

"Sounds like you got out just in time." The inspector turned to Larsen. "What do you want to bet that's the money from the bank heist in Trimble?"

"How much money would you estimate you found?" Larsen asked Dusty.

"Hmm. Large bags filled with bills in small denominations."

"How many bags?"

"I didn't count or anything, but maybe ten or more…"

"Could be millions," Inspector Baxter said. Larsen gave a long low whistle. "How many men can we round up in five minutes to head out there, Sergeant?"

"Eight or ten, I think," said Larsen. "If I call in those deputies to help in emergencies."

Baxter nodded. "What say you go round them up while I get some more info from Dusty here?"

"Okay. I'll make some calls."

● ● ●

Fifteen minutes later, a number of police vehicles were parked out front of Duggan Printing, blocking off the entire street. Officers were hauling out the bags and loading them into the vehicles.

Dusty and Inspector Baxter stood inside the room where they'd found all the money, though it was almost empty at this point.

"You say you've been in this building twice?" Baxter asked Dusty. He pointed down the corridor. "What's down that way?"

"A bunch of empty rooms with bars in the windows. That hall gave me the creeps and I didn't get very far."

"Well, maybe we should check it out. What do you say?"

"Could we bring a few officers with us?" Dusty asked.

"Sure, let's go find some."

They made their way back to the large room and stopped when they suddenly heard a shout from one of the other officers.

"There he goes!"

Dusty caught sight of a figure running along the far side of the ballroom with two officers in hot pursuit. Suddenly a door Dusty had never seen before opened. Sunlight flashed in his eyes, and just like that the fleeing suspect was gone.

CHAPTER
TWENTY-SEVEN

CRACKERS STARED INTENTLY AT GRIMSBY, who had just come into his office. "Tell me again. You were at Duggan Printing and *what* happened?"

"I thought I heard voices down the hall in the direction of the restrooms," Grimsby explained. "But I walked down there and out to the front door and no one was in sight. I must have imagined it."

"I doubt that! When you heard the voices, were you walking towards the restrooms or away from them? And why are you so sweaty? You look like you just ran here."

"I wasn't actually walking when I heard the voices, boss. I was—"

"You know what I mean!" Crackers roared.

"Uh... sure, boss. I guess you want to know what direction I was facing... well, I was facing away from the restrooms, but I wasn't walking. I was standing there thinking."

"Yeah right, Grimsby. As if you know how to think." Vi leaned nonchalantly against the wall with her arms crossed.

Crackers tapped a pencil absently on the desk in front of him. "And the room with our two prisoners, was it between you and the restrooms? In other words was it the prisoners you heard talking? Or someone else perhaps?"

"I'm not sure, boss. I honestly can't recall!"

"Can't recall? Or don't want to exert your brain, you feeble-minded buffoon! Now, I'm only going to ask you this once more, Grimsby: why are you so sweaty?"

"I ran here! The police were after me. They showed up and took all our money!"

Crackers leapt from his chair, his eyes wild with rage. Grimsby covered his head with his arms, expecting a tremendous blow.

"So let me get this straight," Crackers snarled. "You thought you heard voices, but instead of calling me you just assumed everything was good and didn't do anything until the police arrived?" His eyes narrowed. "How did you get away? Or did you? Are you working with the police now?" He looked towards Jackson. "Check the window and tell me if you see the police out there."

Jackson ran out of the room, but came back a moment later. "Everything looks normal out there. No sign of the cops out front, boss."

Crackers sat back down, deep in thought. After a moment, he looked up. "It's time to move the prisoners! We'll move them tonight."

"But what if someone spots us like they did last time?" Vi asked. "Wouldn't it look more natural to move them during the day?"

Crackers stood and began pacing the length of the room. "I hate this! I want to grab those two prisoners now, before the police get their hands on them and hook them up with sketch artists and find out what we look like. We won't last a minute in this town once that happens!"

"I hear you, boss," Vi said. "But the police might be waiting for us now. We have to wait."

Crackers looked at her intently. "Maybe you're right. Okay. We move the prisoners at dawn."

"Boss, dawn is around 4:00 a.m. at this time of year," she reminded him. "Maybe we should do it at a more reasonable hour. Say, 7:30? That way it won't look odd if someone sees us, plus the workers in the other warehouses will have started their shifts by then. There's less of a chance someone will see us."

"I'll say this about you, Vi: you've got brains. No doubt about that," Jackson said while munching on a bag of potato chips.

Vi looked at him angrily. "Will you stop chomping on those chips!"

"I like it, Vi," Crackers decided. "Okay, we'll do this at 7:30. Maybe the police stakeout team will have fallen asleep. Or they may be drowsy and miss us... since a relief team isn't likely to arrive until

8:00. All right. Let's meet here at 7:15 to get everything prepped. Then we'll scout out the building, and if there's no sign of the police we grab the prisoners and run."

"Where are we going to take them, boss?" Grimsby asked.

Crackers smiled. "I have a house that should be perfect. There are bedrooms in the basement, plus a full bathroom and a laundry room. They'll be self-sufficient and we won't need to babysit them. And the basement windows are small enough that no one but a child could crawl out." He reached for his jacket, hung on the back of his office chair. "Let's go over there now. We need to prepare the place... board up the windows so they can't tap on the glass to alert the neighbors. We can nail a sheet of plywood over the door to the basement, too, so they can't open it. Meeting adjourned. Let's head out, people!"

He was about to head out of the room when he stopped and turned to Jackson.

"Oh yeah, a few more things," the boss added. "Clean off your shirt, Jackson. You're covered in crumbs! And Vi, I want you to go find that guy Dusty and keep an eye on him. Find out whatever you can about him." Finally, he looked at Grimsby. "You need to shower. You stink! Make it quick and then meet us over there."

CHAPTER
TWENTY-EIGHT

"WHAT DO YOU MEAN, YOU lost him?" Sergeant Larsen hollered.

The two officers who had chased the suspect at Duggan Printing stood at attention, looking overheated from their chase. They were slightly overweight, and out of shape to boot.

Dusty had gotten a ride back to the police station and watched the two officers get chewed out.

"How is it that you two lost a suspect on foot who looked more overweight than you?" Larsen demanded, standing close to his desk. He ran his fingers through his hair, looking flushed and very upset. Then he took a step backwards. "Now how are we supposed to find out who these people are that robbed the bank in Trimble?"

He said the last part much more softly and sank down into his chair, as if he didn't have the strength to stand anymore. He swiveled towards his desk, rested his elbows on it, and lowered his head into his hands.

The taller of the two officers broke from attention and put his hand on his boss's shoulder. "We'll find them, boss. The suspect was a lot faster than he looked. A lot!"

Inspector Baxter pulled Dusty aside. "We didn't get a chance to search the rest of the building for some sign of your friends, or any sign that they had been there."

"Perhaps we could go look tomorrow after I'm finished at work."

"Can't do it, son. We have to transport that money back to the bank—or rather, the casino who was simply storing their money there while making repairs to their vault. It's a four-hour drive to Trimble.

Each way. We don't have an armored vehicle, so we'll have to use several cruisers full of officers to make a show of force. Five million dollars is a lot of money and a big temptation. We'll post an officer at Duggan Printing round the clock until we can search it for your friends. Unfortunately, we're going to be spread pretty thin. I'm sorry to say this, but we'll have to wait until the following day to search for your friends."

Dusty didn't look too happy about having to wait.

Baxter turned to Larsen. "Why don't you and your men search Duggan Printing tomorrow and we'll all meet here the day after?"

Larsen, his head still in his hands, shrugged. "Sure, we can do that."

"If you find Dusty's friends, call his hotel and leave a message for him."

"Of course," Larsen mumbled.

Dusty nodded. "All right. I'll pop in after work on Wednesday if I don't hear anything before then."

"Wednesday it is." The inspector clapped Dusty on the back, then strode to Larsen's desk.

With that, Dusty headed for the door and once out on the sidewalk decided to walk to the diner and fill Cindy in on the day's events.

While crossing the street to the diner, he noticed a petite woman sitting on the bench across from the diner. She seemed to be eyeing the establishment rather closely—but when she spied Dusty, she became suddenly transfixed by something in her purse.

Dusty didn't like the looks of her. That was the same bench the overweight man had watched him from.

Once inside, he led Cindy to a booth from which they could see the woman.

"Don't make it obvious," he said, "but do you see that woman on the bench across the street?"

She nodded while trying to look without turning her head much.

"Have you ever seen her before?" Dusty asked. "Oh man, what if that loan shark has finally found me? I don't have his money yet!"

Cindy turned her full attention on Dusty and put her hand over his. "Don't worry so much. I've seen her around before, so she's not a spy for this loan shark—not unless he planted her here two years before you arrived. You know, just on the off-chance you were going to run and wind up here."

Dusty smiled ruefully and breathed a big sigh of relief. "Oh, thank goodness. You're right. I need to stop stressing over things, or I'm going to give myself a heart attack."

Cindy patted his hand gently.

"But who is she then, and why is she watching the diner? That other man I saw was sitting in the exact same spot there... and he was clearly watching me."

"Why don't we go ask her?" Cindy said mischievously.

"You mean go right out there and walk up to her?"

"Yeah. Come on." Jumping out of her seat, she grabbed Dusty by the hand and pulled him to his feet. "It'll be fun!"

They calmed down and walked nonchalantly to the door and stepped outside. Dusty wondered what the woman would do when she realized she'd been spotted.

But he didn't wonder for very long. The bench was empty.

CHAPTER
TWENTY-NINE

WHEN DUSTY ARRIVED AT THE warehouse the next day, Jerry met him by the entrance. "The forklift has a flat!" he said coldly. "You can clean my private bathroom while it's being repaired. Follow me."

Jerry led him to his own office and showed him his restroom. Dusty took a peek into the room. It looked beyond disgusting. The toilet had overflowed, there was toilet paper and paper towels on the floor, and it looked like a whole roll of toilet paper was floating in the toilet, along with other debris. The smell was off the charts.

Great, he thought. *Just great!*

Jerry watched as Dusty viewed the pitiful state of the restroom. "I want to see this room so clean that you'll be happy eating your lunch in there," he said with a smirk on his face.

Dusty looked at him quickly, hoping he was joking. But there was no humor on his face.

What does this guy have against me?

Once Jerry had shown Dusty the restroom, he went to work in his office and Dusty was left in the bathroom choking on the fumes.

Red found him there at break time. "Wow. That looks nasty!"

Dusty glared at him.

"Don't lose heart, pal," Red said. "Just hang on until lunch. Then I'll give you a hand. We'll have this place looking brand new in no time."

"Do you have a gas mask?" Dusty croaked.

"Fresh out, partner. But don't worry. Lunch time will be here before you know it and then your misery will be almost at an end."

"What if Jerry doesn't leave the office? He does that sometimes."

"I happen to know that Jerry's wife and kids are coming to take him out for lunch."

Red left Dusty taking small, tiny breaths because of the horrific odors.

He steeled himself for the nasty job ahead, then went to town on the toilet with the plunger. As he'd suspected, a whole toilet paper roll had been stuffed to the bottom of the bowl. Dusty could feel fury rising inside him; the toilet had been plugged deliberately.

Finally lunch came and Jerry left, as promised. No sooner was he gone than Red was there with rubber gloves, a face mask, and a shower cap.

"Nice look!" Dusty teased. "But why didn't you offer me any of those?"

"Sorry, there wasn't enough for two," his friend replied through the face mask. He pulled the mask down. "But you got the toilet unclogged and it smells much better in here."

"At least it's bearable now. We still need to scrub the floor, though, so give me a hand and the rest should be relatively easy."

Soon they were finished and stepped back to admire the sparkling bathroom. The toilet gleamed.

"This bathroom hasn't looked this clean in years!" Red said.

"You use this bathroom regularly, do you?"

"Not regularly, but any time Jerry's gone and the other restroom is occupied, we come use this one."

"Jerry must be gone quite often then…"

"It happens more than you might think." Red winked. "Now, let's hurry and get these cleaning supplies put away so we can go eat lunch."

Dusty gave him a surprised look. "We still have time to eat? I didn't think I'd want to eat for days after first seeing the mess in here, but I'm starving!"

"We sure do, but only fifteen minutes."

They grabbed up the cleaning supplies with the mop and plunger and hurried out.

After eating they walked out to the main warehouse where Dusty noticed that the flat tire on the forklift had been fixed.

"That guy is going too far," Dusty said darkly.

"What do you mean?"

"I have no proof, but if we had video of this whole place I'm positive it would show Jerry letting the air out of the tires this morning then going to his private restroom and jamming a roll of paper as far into the toilet as he could get it. Then he did his business, flushing, and came to wait for me to show up so he could make me clean it up."

"He really pushed a whole roll of toilet paper down there so the toilet would back up?"

"He sure did!"

Red looked around nervously. "Let's talk about this some other time. Jerry might be back any second." He lowered his voice. "In fact, he already might be back and listening to us."

Dusty fired up the forklift and got back to work. He had only been working a few minutes when he heard his name being called. He shut down the forklift and looked around. Spying Jerry, he got out and walked over to him.

"I thought I told you to finish that bathroom," Jerry said.

"It is finished. Didn't you look?"

Jerry glared at him. "It better be or you'll wish you'd never met me."

CHAPTER
THIRTY

AFTER WORK, DUSTY RETURNED TO the diner to see Cindy and have a cold drink.

"Lemonade?" Cindy asked after she had seated him in what was becoming his usual seat.

"Can you recommend anything else?"

"We mostly just serve coffee. This isn't a fancy restaurant, you know." Cindy winked. "If you want something cold, how about I get you some ice water?"

"Sounds good."

Cindy smiled. "Coming right up." She turned around and skipped off to the counter.

When Cindy brought the water over to the table, he took a deep drink. "Wow! That's good."

Cindy laughed. "I'm glad you like it. So how was your day?"

"It was horrible!" Dusty was about to tell her all the details when the diner door opened and a group of people entered.

Cindy raised a finger. "Hold that thought."

She rushed off to serve the newcomers.

For a while, the place was busy. Dusty sipped his ice water and watched Cindy move between the front counter, the kitchen, and a few of the booths, serving everyone their food.

Eventually things slowed down and the place was empty again. Cindy came over to Dusty's table and plunked herself down opposite him.

"Okay," she said. "Now continue your story of why today was horrible."

Dusty told her about the flat tire on his forklift and his ordeal of having to clean the bathroom. Angrily he told the part about finding a roll of paper wedged into the bottom of the toilet.

"Are you serious?" Cindy said.

"Yes! I'm sure Jerry let the air out of the tire, then stuffed that roll of toilet paper into the toilet before doing his business It was horribly disgusting."

"This isn't good. Maybe I should talk to my father about this."

"Please, don't get him involved. I haven't seen him once since he hired me, and if he talks to Jerry, it will only make things worse. I'm sure if I keep my head low and avoid Jerry as much as possible, things will calm down and get better."

"Okay. But if things don't get better soon, you must let me speak to my father about this. This isn't right."

"Deal," Dusty said holding out his hand.

Cindy shook his proffered hand to seal the arrangement. Her hand was warm and soft to the touch and Dusty felt all tingly inside.

CHAPTER
THIRTY-ONE

DUSTY WAS FILLED WITH EXCITEMENT and anticipation. This was the day he was to go with the police to look around Duggan Printing for Charlie and Tina.

Work seemed to drag by, but eventually the shift ended. Dusty couldn't get out of the warehouse fast enough.

"Why are you in such a hurry?" Red asked at one point. He smiled when Dusty told him the plans for the rest of the day. "Sounds exciting. I hope you find your friends."

Dusty exited the warehouse and noticed police cars at Duggan Printing. Thinking that Inspector Baxter and Squid Larsen must be over there, he walked briskly over.

He found the inspector talking to one of the officers.

"Ah, Dusty, glad you noticed us," said Baxter. "Seems all has been quiet here... no one going in or out. We're just about to breach the building and search for your friends. Care to join us?"

"You bet. If all these officers are going in with you, I'm game."

The inspector nodded and headed to the door of the building.

Dusty followed.

The door was locked, so everyone waited while an officer jimmied the door. A moment later they were in.

"Let's allow the other officers to go in first, shall we?" Baxter said to Dusty, pulling him off to the side so the other men could get by.

There were six men in all and Dusty was happy to let the four officers go ahead.

"I take it Sergeant Larsen wasn't able to come here yesterday to search?" Dusty asked.

"Unfortunately no," Baxter replied. "A bunch of youths caught shoplifting had him busy all day. He had to meet with them and each of their parents. Most of his men were tied up with us or guarding this place."

"I figured something had come up when I didn't hear from him yesterday."

Soon they had passed through the large makeshift ballroom and entered the hallway at the back. The four officers looked in every room while Dusty hung back with the inspector.

It wasn't until they were near the end of the hall that one of the officers found something.

"Sir, I think you'll want to see this room," the officer said.

When Dusty came in behind Baxter, he saw a room much larger than the others. The floor was littered with empty cans of pop, bottles of water, and food containers. It was a complete mess.

"What happened here?" Dusty asked.

"If you ask me, looks like someone has been locked in here for a couple weeks," Baxter said.

Dusty noticed a second room off to the side and discovered an attached bathroom. "Did any of the other rooms have a full bath?"

"Not any of the rooms we checked," said a stocky officer with blonde hair and a moustache with a reddish tinge to it.

"I wonder why this room does then. Plus, this room has no window in the door."

A second officer nodded. "I heard growing up that this was once a mental ward."

"Probably the administrator lived in this room," the inspector suggested as he ran his hands through his hair.

Dusty noticed it was rather hot with everyone crowded into the small space, so he walked back out into the hall to let the officers do their thing.

A few minutes later, the inspector came out of the room with two officers in tow. "Your friends were definitely in there," Baxter said.

"How do you know?" Dusty asked.

"We found some words scratched on the wall behind one of the beds. We couldn't see it until we pulled the bed away from the wall, but it said 'Charlie & Tina were here.'"

CHAPTER
THIRTY-TWO

"SO HAVE YOU HEARD THE weather forecast for this weekend?" Red asked at lunch the next day before taking a bite of his sandwich.

"Uh, no. Why?"

"It doesn't look good. I mean, it was supposed to be a nice weekend, perfect for going out, but now they're forecasting rain all weekend. But don't worry."

"I'm not worried."

"Oh, you looked a bit disgusted or something when I said we couldn't go to Floggin's Bog this weekend."

"That was me looking relieved, actually."

"In that case, I'd strongly suggest you work on your expressions."

After work, Dusty headed to the diner. It was becoming a routine, he realized. Obviously he wanted to see Cindy, but he wondered why he had come to like seeing her so much.

When he entered the diner, there were only a few customers and Cindy was serving one of them. He noticed a familiar face in a booth near the back. It was Inspector Baxter, probably drinking his coffee again. Shouldn't he be out trying to locate Charlie and Tina?

Oh well, he thought. *Perhaps he's just taking a break from the search.*

He put it out of his mind as Cindy came up to him. "Have you read today's newspaper?" she asked.

Dusty looked up into her anxious face. "No…"

"You've got to see this. Just wait, let me grab you a coffee and my copy of the paper." She hurried to the counter and disappeared into the kitchen.

A moment later, she reappeared carrying a newspaper. She handed Dusty his coffee and plunked it down, sitting on the bit of empty seat beside him.

"Move over," she said.

He slid over and she moved closer to get more comfortable while flipping pages of the paper.

"Here it is!" she proclaimed.

Dusty leaned over and directed his gaze to where her finger was pointing. The headline fairly jumped out at him.

LOCAL MAN FINDS STOLEN BANK LOOT

Two months ago, $5 million was stolen from the bank in Trimble, Saskatchewan. Two days ago, a young man new to our fair town found that money and directed the police to it.

The money has all been returned to the bank, who in turn returned it to its rightful owner: the casino. It seems the casino had offered a ten percent reward to whoever provided police with the information leading to the return of the money.

Our very own Dusty Burns will be the happy recipient of that reward money.

The article went on to contain statements from the police saying that Dusty was looking for his friends. There wasn't anything written about Charlie and Tina that Dusty didn't already know, so he quickly lost interest.

He looked at Cindy with an unspoken question on his lips.

"Don't you see what this means?" she asked.

"Not really."

"I may be guessing here, but maybe Charlie and Tina saw something they weren't supposed to see and that's why they disappeared. It looks like Crackers is behind it, and now that you're mentioned in the paper maybe he'll want to make you disappear too."

"Do you think they might... not be alive?"

"I really... don't know," she said. "But Dusty, what if Crackers sees this newspaper? He probably already knows you're looking for

Charlie and Tina, but now he'll know you were the one who led the police to the money."

Dusty looked at her blankly.

"Don't you see, Dusty? When Crackers reads this, he may want revenge for the money he feels was his. You've got to lay low."

A light went off in Dusty's head. "He'll come looking for me! But how do I lay low? I'm sure Crackers or someone associated with him trashed my hotel room, so they already know where I'm staying."

"We can figure something out. Maybe you can stay with my dad."

Dusty recalled the man and the woman who had been watching the diner for him. "I'm pretty sure they know my connection with you, as well as my job at the warehouse. They'd look at your dad's place pretty quickly." He snapped his fingers. "Maybe Red will let me stay with him."

"That's an excellent idea. Gus, he's the cook here, sometimes lets me use his car. I could maybe give you a lift to the hotel to get your things and then drive you to Red's."

"I'm sure I'll be okay walking back to the hotel. I can talk to Red tomorrow and see if I can say there."

"But this article," she said, tapping the newspaper. "What if Crackers comes looking for you and catches you alone on foot?"

Dusty saw movement outside and turned to look just in time to see three people marching up the sidewalk towards the diner. Crackers was in the middle. With a sinister face like his, Dusty recognized Crackers immediately. The man had his hair cropped short, and the skin stretched tight across his face that sent cold shivers up and down his spine.

Then Dusty noticed the man on Crackers's right.

"Uh-oh," Dusty said. "Here comes Crackers, and the guy beside him is the same man I saw sitting on the bench across the street the other day. And the woman is the same one who was watching us." Suddenly, relief flooded over him. "But if those two are with Crackers, it means they aren't from the loan shark. The Grub hasn't found me!"

Cindy jumped up, grabbed Dusty's arm, and dragged him out of his seat. "Come on! You can celebrate later. We have to get you out of here right now."

As Dusty got up, he noticed that the good inspector was no longer in the diner. He'd been so focused on what Cindy was telling him that he hadn't even noticed the man leave.

All this went through his mind in a split second. Then he noticed his coffee still sitting untouched.

"But my coffee! It'll get cold."

"Forget your coffee. Let's go!"

Cindy took Dusty by the collar and practically dragged him down the aisle of the diner towards the counter. They ducked to remain out of sight.

"Joe," Cindy said to the customer sitting right at the counter, "if anyone comes in looking for this man, he left through the front door just a few minutes ago. Okay?"

Joe nodded his head without even looking up.

Cindy pulled Dusty after her as she led the way through the kitchen, where Gus the cook was busy in front of the stove.

Then they were out the back door. They turned and fled.

Dusty had never been behind the diner and nothing looked familiar as they raced through yards and around corners. When he was good and lost, they entered a backyard and Cindy led Dusty to a shed. She pulled a key from her pocket and unlocked the padlock.

"I'm going to lock the door behind you in case Crackers and his pals manage to track us this far," she said breathlessly. "They won't think you're in here if the padlock is on. I'll come back for you when I'm sure the coast is clear. Don't make a sound until you hear my voice, though. Do you understand?"

Dusty nodded.

Cindy leaned forward and gave him a tiny kiss on the lips, then spun him around and gave him a gentle push into the shed.

He had to stoop to enter the low structure. He spied a small window on the wall opposite the door. The sun had been behind him to the south as he'd entered, so the window had to be facing north.

When the door closed, Dusty was left in semi-darkness. The window was covered in dirt and grime, but it still let in enough light so Dusty could tell he was in a garden shed. He saw a lawnmower, a couple of rakes, a watering can, and a bunch of ceramic planters of various sizes in a haphazard pile. He also found a spot to sit and tried to make himself comfortable by leaning again the lawnmower, his knees drawn up to his chest. He found it pretty crowded, but it was the best he could do.

He wondered if this was Cindy's shed and if she used these planters. Did she push this mower around the yard on warm days? Then he thought about the kiss and felt a rush of feelings for Cindy that he hadn't felt before.

His thoughts drifted to their first meeting and how she had flopped into the seat opposite him. The recollection made him smile.

But what he liked most about Cindy was how eager she was to help him. First she'd helped him find a job. Then she had been eager to help in any way to find Charlie and Tina. Dusty hadn't wanted her poking around on her own, but she had gone with him to meet Mrs. Wilcox...

Thinking of Mrs. Wilcox caused him to recall her huge Bible. He was still amazed that she used that book as a mirror for her own life, not to use it to get others to change their behavior. Most interesting.

Next, his thoughts jumped to Inspector Baxter. Why did the man seem more interested in his coffee than finding Charlie and Tina? It was beginning to irritate him. He saw the inspector in the diner almost every day, and today would have been a good day to have him around, when Crackers and his pals showed up. But he'd left prior to their arrival.

He must have dozed off, because the next thing he knew he heard a key in the lock and the sound of the padlock being removed.

As the door opened, bright sunlight flooded in and blinded Dusty. A shadow loomed over him, but he couldn't see who was standing in the doorway. Was it Crackers? Or one of his pals? Had they caught Cindy, gotten the key off her, and forced her to tell them where he was?

"Well, silly, are you going to sit there just staring at me? Or are you wanting to come out?" Cindy laughed.

Relief overwhelmed him. Dusty struggled to his feet. His muscles were so tight from sitting squashed in the shed that he stumbled out on stiff legs. He must have been in there longer than he'd thought.

He gave Cindy a big hug.

"It's good to see you too," Cindy said.

"What took so long?"

"Customers. Now come on, let's go."

CHAPTER
THIRTY-THREE

ON THE WALK BACK TO the diner, Dusty asked, "What happened while I was sitting in the shed?"

"Crackers and his pals were gone by the time I got back, but Joe said they came in and asked where you were. When he told them you had just left, they rushed outside and didn't return."

"That's it?"

Cindy laughed. "Well, Joe said he tried not to look. He was acting unconcerned. Guess he's read a lot of novels and wanted to try his hand at acting like a spy."

"So Crackers didn't notice my coffee sitting on the table?"

"I really don't know. Joe said they looked around a moment before asking about you. But even if they had seen your coffee and noticed the steam rising from it, it would have just added to the fact that'd you'd left in a hurry."

They had arrived at the diner by then and went in through the kitchen. Gus was still busy at the stove.

Cindy went over to the cook and whispered something in his ear. Then Gus reached into his pocket, pulled out some keys, and handed them to Cindy. She smiled and gave Gus a quick peck on the cheek.

With a bounce in her step, she came back, took Dusty by the arm, and led him through the rest of the kitchen to the main counter. Pretty soon they were walking outside again, this time through the front door.

"What was that all about with Gus?" Dusty asked.

"I'm going to drive you home."

"In Gus's car?"

"You bet. I figure with Crackers and those other two looking for you, it wouldn't be safe for you to walk home right now."

Dusty looked left up the street but didn't see a single car.

"So where is it?" he asked.

"Right there, silly," Cindy giggled while pointing to the right.

Dusty turned and saw a blue pickup truck parked alone at the curb. He smacked his forehead with the heel of his hand. "I can't believe I didn't see it there."

Just as they were approaching the truck, an elderly woman came out of the nearby bakery and stood in front of them.

"Well, hello, you two," she said. "Dusty and Cindy, right?"

Dusty looked a little more closely and recognized the woman right away. It was Mrs. Wilcox, Crackers's ex-wife.

"Have you found your two friends yet?" Mrs. Wilcox asked.

"Almost," he told her. "They were in a back room at Duggan Printing, but the police figure we missed them by a day or so."

"Oh dear, that's too bad. Now, I've been hoping to run into one or both of you. I'd like to invite the two of you to come to church with me. What do you say?"

"To be honest, I don't—"

"We'd love to," Cindy said.

Mrs. Wilcox clapped her hands together and squealed with glee. "How lovely. I'm so excited." She looked at Cindy. "You know where Duggan Community Church is, don't you, dear?"

"Yes, I sure do," Cindy said with a smile.

"Then I hope to see you both there very soon. Now, I must be off home before the baked goodies dry out."

She held up a bag holding her latest purchases. Dusty thought he smelled fresh danishes.

Mrs. Wilcox waved and walked briskly down the sidewalk.

"Now why did you..." Dusty said.

Cindy put a finger to his lips. "Shh, we'll talk later. I have to hurry and get you home, then come back before the supper rush begins.

Veronika, who normally works the evening shift, is sick today and I need to help out Gus."

She unlocked the truck door for Dusty, then went around to the driver's side and got in.

The drive was short and soon Dusty was back at his hotel talking to Tom and Wendy. When he spotted a newspaper on the front desk, it was a simple matter to flip to the correct page and let them read the article.

"I need to go someplace else for a while and lay low," he explained after they'd read it. "Someplace where this gang can't find me. I wouldn't be safe here anymore."

"Au contraire," Tom insisted. "We had a security system installed after the break-in. No one can get in here now without the police arriving to arrest them."

Dusty stared at them for a while. "So it's actually safe for me to stay?"

"Absolutely," Wendy said. "But if it will make you feel better, we can move you to a different room so no one knows exactly where you are."

"That might help me sleep more soundly at night."

Tom smiled. "Done."

"But if I stay here, I still have the problem of getting to work safely. It may not be smart to get around on foot right now."

Tom and Wendy looked at each other, and it seemed like they came to a decision without uttering a word.

"We'll drive you," Tom said.

"I couldn't accept that. I don't want to be an imposition."

"It's no bother," Wendy insisted. "I go by your work practically every day to do pickups from our food supplier."

Dusty raised his eyebrows. He knew Tom and Wendy really liked him, but he suspected they were going out of their way to help him now.

"Okay, I accept," Dusty said, feeling a bit sheepish.

"It's settled then. We'll get you into a new room right away and Wendy will drive you to work in the morning."

CHAPTER
THIRTY-FOUR

DUSTY WOKE UP FEELING RESTED and refreshed. He did a big stretch, then leaped out of bed and headed to the shower.

Later, while finishing a sumptuous breakfast consisting of over-easy eggs with toast and fried ham, Wendy appeared at his table.

"I'm just going to get the car and bring it around," she said. "I'll meet you outside in five minutes."

"Perfect," Dusty said, wiping his mouth with his napkin.

He got up from the table and went into the kitchen to get the pre-prepared lunch that the staff had been getting ready for him every day.

Afterwards he headed for the front door and waited a few minutes for Wendy to drive up. He hopped in the passenger seat.

"Buckle up." Wendy put the car in gear and they were off. "How are you enjoying being a forklift driver?"

"It's okay. There's always a little variety to keep the day interesting."

"Well, that's good to hear. Now, just relax. We'll be there before you know it. What time do you get off work?"

"Usually about one o'clock."

"I'll see you around one o'clock then."

"What? Wait. I'm sure I can catch a ride home from someone at work."

Just then, Wendy arrived at the warehouse. She stopped the car and turned in her seat. "Don't be silly. It's a two-minute drive."

Dusty didn't want to be late, so he dropped his protest and got out.

"Thanks for the lift."

With that, he casually strolled into the warehouse and stopped short, surprised to see Cindy's father, Tony, talking with Jerry, Red, and the two pickers, Tim and Warren.

Jerry glared at Dusty when he saw him.

"Dusty, could you come join us please?" Tony called out.

Dusty wondered what was up. He didn't have to wonder long.

"The 1970 Martin D35 guitar is missing!" Jerry yelled at him. "Where did you hide it, you sniveling little thief?"

Taken aback, Dusty didn't know what to say at first.

"Now Jerry," Tony said, "we don't know yet who has taken it."

"When did it disappear?" Dusty asked.

Jerry seemed livid. "We found it gone this morning!"

"So it could have disappeared anytime then."

"No, we saw it yesterday when we were working," said Warren.

"So it went missing between yesterday and this morning," Dusty said. "Well, I went straight from here to the diner yesterday and then got a ride to the hotel. If I'd taken it, Cindy would have seen it."

"Now, Dusty, no one's pointing fingers here." Tony looked pointedly at Jerry. "Right, Jerry?" Then he addressed the rest of the group. "We just want to know if anyone saw anything. The musician who stores his equipment here pays us very well to keep it safe and we'll lose his business if we can't find it before he comes looking. That's all for now, so let's all go to work. Jerry, I have to run out of town on business. Can I depend on you to let me know the minute this guitar is found?"

"Yes, sir!"

While Jerry walked Tony to the door, Dusty got onto the forklift and started loading pallets. He had just started when he heard his name called again. He looked around and spied Jerry waving at him.

He shut off the forklift and walked over.

"I have another job for you right now," Jerry said.

"I'm right in the middle of loading pallets. The trucks are waiting. Can't this wait?"

Jerry grew red in the face. "No, it can't!" he snapped.

"So who is going to finish the loading?"

"Just you never mind about that! I'll find someone. Now follow me and I'll show you what I need you to do."

• • •

Dusty looked aghast at the dirty bathroom just off Jerry's office. The toilet was full and overflowing. It looked almost the same as the last time he'd been told to clean it.

"You can't be serious," Dusty said. "Did you clog it with a roll of toilet paper again?"

Jerry just smirked and left the office, heading back towards the main warehouse.

Dusty found the supplies Red had used the last time and got to work. It was messy, nasty work and he wished he was getting that reward money soon so he could quit this job and get out from under Jerry's thumb. But he didn't know how long it might take for the reward money to come. It could be months, and in the meantime he still needed a paycheck so he could afford to stay at the hotel and eat.

At break time, Dusty had just finished cleaning the putrid bathroom when Jerry strolled in.

"Oh good, you're almost done," Jerry said. "You can do the one by the break room next."

"Oh good!" Dusty replied sarcastically.

He walked slowly over to the break room, so Jerry would know that he wasn't doing this willingly. He bumped into Red just outside the bathrooms. Red was just coming out and seemed to be in a big hurry.

"I wouldn't go in there if I were you," Red said.

"It's not like I have a choice! By the way, who has been running the forklift in my absence?"

"Good ol' Jerry."

"So how do you find it telling your boss which truck to put which pallet on?"

"No fun at all. Every time I tell him what to do, he glares at me." Red shook his head in disgust. "You want some help on this bathroom?"

"I thought you said I shouldn't go in there... why would you want to go back in?"

"I wouldn't do it for myself, but I'd do it for a friend."

"That's mighty kind of you." Dusty grinned. "Well, come on then. Here, you better take the rubber gloves and the face mask."

"Why do you say that?"

"The way you bolted out of the bathroom just now. Something tells me you're going to need them more than I am."

Red donned the face mask and was just putting on the gloves when Dusty pushed open the bathroom door.

• • •

Just before the lunch break, the bathroom door opened and the two came out. Dusty noticed that Red was looking a little green.

"How is it that you look fine after what we just saw in there?" Red asked.

"I guess I'm just getting desensitized. Remember, this is the second time Jerry has had me clean the bathroom. Do you recall how I looked the first time?"

Red laughed. "Yeah, I sure do."

A few minutes later, they were sitting in the break room with their lunches in front of them. Red was looking a lot better, now that they were in the fresh air, devoid of horrible smells and ghastly sights.

Just then, Jerry entered. Dusty and Red looked up in surprise because Jerry normally ate in his office; he was very rarely seen in the break room.

"Are you finished with the restrooms?" Jerry asked gruffly.

"Yes, I am," Dusty said.

"Good. You can start sweeping the warehouse as soon as lunch is over."

"Don't you have others to do that?"

Jerry glared at him. "I've had just about enough of your insubordination. The warehouse needs sweeping, so sweep it! Unless you'd rather find another job."

Jerry turned and stomped off.

Once he was out of earshot, Dusty groaned. "It'll take days and days to sweep this place. It's huge."

"Actually, it's a small warehouse compared to some," Red said. "We've only got ten thousand square feet. I've seen some that were the size of a football field, close to sixty thousand square feet. And those aren't even the big ones."

Dusty rested his face in his hands. "Thanks. I feel so much better now."

"I think I know what you need: some time out of town, somewhere to take your mind off work and relax. Thankfully, tomorrow's Saturday. We could go to Floggin's Bog. The forecast's changed. Rain is still expected for the afternoon, but the morning is supposed to be nice. What do you say?"

"I guess that sounds okay," Dusty said into his hands.

CHAPTER
THIRTY-FIVE

DUSTY AMBLED ALONG A SHADY path through the trees at Floggin's Bog with Red and Dusty, with Red's dog Rex walking out in front of them. Signs had been posted periodically with images of trees and other plants, explaining more about them.

Dusty didn't find any of it very interesting, so he didn't pay much attention. That is, until they came to one very peculiar sign. *"The dog gnawed the log right here at the bog,"* it read.

"What is that doing here?" Dusty asked.

"Oh," Red said, smiling. "When my grandfather ran this place, he liked to make up silly little songs. He posted some of them here when he started the preserve."

Cindy laughed. "That's hilarious."

After they'd been walking for a while, they came across a bench. Cindy sat down.

"What are we supposed to see if we sit here?" she asked.

Red sat down next to her. Just ahead was a small clearing bordered by aspen trees. There were evergreens and the odd elm, but it was mostly aspens.

"It's here so you can take a break and enjoy the greenery," Red explained. "Sorry, I'm not an expert on plants and can't describe everything you'll see. But throughout the nature preserve you'll find saskatoon berries, pin cherries, choke cherries, and gooseberries. Also poplar, lilac, laurel, and willow trees. Not all of it is visible from this bench, but they're scattered around. Oh, and if you see any three-leaved plants with one large leaf and two smaller ones, don't touch it. It could be poison ivy."

"And here I thought Poison Ivy was just a character from the comics," Dusty said.

As Cindy enjoyed the view, she pointed to another sign with an unusual poem written on it:

> Once upon a time in a land called Bog
> I met a man who had a dog
> When that dog turned three years old
> He dug in the ground and he found gold.

"That is so cute," she said. "Did your grandfather write these himself?"

Red nodded. "Yes. My mom said she grew up laughing at these short funny poems."

They soon continued walking, and Dusty noticed that the path changed under their feet, going from dirt to gravel. At one point, they even crossed a raised wooden walkway, built up to traverse some swampy ground. On the other side, they came back down onto a narrow graveled path with a curve in the trail ahead.

"Oh, look!" Cindy called from up ahead. "There's more people here today, but it might be a bit tough to pass each other on this narrow stretch."

When Dusty could see around the bend, he saw an overweight man in a dumpy trench coat alongside the same slim, attractive woman he'd seen with Crackers approaching the diner.

"It's Crackers's people," he hissed.

"Uh-oh," Red said as the pair coming towards them pulled out guns.

Dusty dove into the bush as bullets flew around them. He dimly heard Rex barking as he sailed through the air.

When he landed, he crawled deeper into the woods and met up with Cindy behind a large elm tree.

"Are you okay?" he whispered.

"Yes. Are you okay?"

Dusty nodded. Bullets were still pinging off trees, but landing nowhere close to where they hid.

"Have you seen Red?" Dusty asked.

"I think he dove into the bush on the opposite side of the trail."

After a few minutes, Dusty realized that the shooting had stopped. He signaled to Cindy, then made his way as quietly as he could back to the trail. When he peeked out of the bush, he saw no one on the trail except Rex, who was still barking.

"Rex must have scared those people off," Cindy said.

Red didn't stop barking until he saw Dusty and Cindy come out of hiding. He then whined and headed into the bush on the opposite side of the trail, looking back occasionally as if to see if the humans were following.

"Help!" someone called out.

"That sounded like Red," Dusty said.

They looked around but couldn't see him through all the bushes. Red kept calling for him, though, and they followed the direction of his voice.

They burst through a thicket of tangled vines and rose bushes to find Red stuck in a bog.

"I'm sinking," Red said, frantically trying to get back to shore.

"Stop struggling!" Dusty said. "Try to stay still while we figure out how to pull you out. How'd you end up in there?"

"Bullets were getting awfully close as I ran through the bush and I wasn't watching where I was going. I fell in here."

Dusty reached out to him. "Try to grab my hand."

Red stretched his hand out while trying not to move his body, but Dusty couldn't quite reach him.

"Cindy, come hold on to me. I think I can reach Red if I can reach a little farther."

Cindy grabbed a handful of Dusty's shirt, then tried as best she could to brace herself. She crouched to lower her center of gravity and spread her legs, leaning away from Dusty.

Dusty stretched towards Red, but their fingers were still two inches apart. He tried stretching further by leaning a little farther.

"Dusty, your shirt is slipping through my fingers," Cindy said, sounding worried. "I can't hold on."

"Just a little further." Dusty leaned a little bit more, straining to grab Red's hand.

Suddenly he was falling. He landed right near the shore and Cindy quickly pulled him out.

"Eww, you smell," Cindy said, holding her nose.

"Find something to pull me out with," Red said, still trying to remain still. But even so, he was slowly sinking. The bog had come up to his chest.

Dusty looked around, but all he saw were prickly rose bushes, tall grass, and the odd twig. He headed deeper into the trees.

"Hurry, Dusty!" Cindy called.

Dusty, urged on by the sound of her cry, moved faster, his eyes darting quickly around. He spied a fallen tree with a limb that was just long enough to get the job done. The limb was already nearly sheared off, so Dusty grabbed it and gave it a quick yank.

Limb in hand, he turned around. Which direction had he come from?

"Cindy!"

"Hurry, Dusty, we don't have much time!"

"Keep talking so I can find you," Dusty hollered. "I have something I think will work."

It took a moment for him to get back to the bog, following the sound of Cindy's voice. Then he pushed the limb out to Red and started to pull.

Still, Red didn't budge.

"Cindy, come help me," Dusty implored.

Together they pulled, and finally Red started to move. Even Rex tried to help by pulling on Dusty's pant leg with his teeth.

Eventually they got Red out, all filthy and dirty from the bog. As bad as he looked, though, he smelled even worse.

"You guys desperately need a shower and a dry set of clothes," Cindy said. She was the only one not covered in the oozy muck.

"I agree." Dusty tried to balance on one leg while attempting to wring some water from his pantleg.

Red, covered in mud and grime, just nodded.

Now that they were safe, they decided to call it a day and head back towards their car. On the way they found a water tap beside the trail. Cindy turned around while Red and Dusty took off their pants, shirts, socks, and shoes and rinsed them off so they wouldn't get Red's car dirty.

"Phew, you guys really reek," Cindy said when they were all in the car. She leaned her head out the window and took large lungfuls of air all the way back to town.

CHAPTER
THIRTY-SIX

CRACKERS STARED AT GRIMSBY, HIS face contorted and red with anger. He didn't say anything, causing Grimsby to sweat from the pressure. He kept dabbing at his face with his handkerchief.

When Crackers did speak, his voice was low and menacing. "You know how you are always wanting to shoot someone, Grimsby? And I keep saying no? Well, I'm one inch away from having you shot. Are we clear on that?"

Peter Grimsby nodded his head vigorously and dabbed at his face.

Crackers turned to Vi. "And you... I thought you knew better than this."

Vi kept her head down. "But boss, they're responsible for taking our money. I thought—"

"A thought never entered your head, Vi! You were acting on emotion, and that could get you killed. Or even worse, thrown in prison for a very long time. Who do you think the police would suspect if, merely days after finding the missing bank loot, the one who is due the reward money was assassinated? I'll tell you who they would suspect: us! And if they ever found us, we would go to jail for bank robbery and murder. Would you enjoy the long sentence the judge would give us, Vi?"

Vi shook her head.

"I'm glad you're using your brain now. Killing this Dusty fellow will not bring the money back, so what's the point?"

"Revenge," Grimsby said.

"Let me ask you this, Grimsby. Would twenty years in prison be worth it for one act of revenge?"

Grimsby mopped his face again with his handkerchief. "Uh, no, I guess not."

"Very good. So you will stay away from this Dusty fellow from this day forward. Is that understood?"

Grimsby nodded.

"But boss, I thought you wanted to get Dusty for taking our money," Jackson said quietly. He had been watching the exchange from a table in the corner.

Crackers turned to the third man in his gang. "Oh yes, you're referring to the day I went to the diner, livid. Well, yes, I was guilty that day of acting on my emotions. So I'm going to let this little incident with Vi and Grimsby slide. Just don't let it happen again. Now, I must say that I do want to repay Dusty Burns for what he's done, but I'm going to think very clearly about it. And when the right moment comes, I will act. I can't trust you clowns not to act rashly, so you will leave this one to me." He smiled with determination. "About the other day, how did you get our prisoners out of Duggan Printing without the police seeing you? Because I heard there was a police cruiser stationed there around the clock."

Vi smiled. "We took them out the back door where we had parked so as not to be seen. There was only one officer there parked at the front."

"You weren't followed?"

"No way, boss," Jackson declared.

"At least you did one thing right. Now go check on our prisoners and get out of my sight."

Grimsby and Vi filed out, shame-faced. Jackson waited a moment, then followed them.

CHAPTER
THIRTY-SEVEN

IT TOOK DUSTY TWO WORKDAYS to sweep the huge warehouse floor. By the time he finished on Tuesday, he had a couple of blisters on his hands and the skin was tender. He felt exhausted.

"Who normally does this job?" he asked Red during one of their breaks.

"Tim and Warren, either before we get here in the morning or after we leave for the day."

"I'm just glad I'm done. Now maybe I can get back to running the forklift."

"That sure would make me happy," Red said. "I'm sick and tired of working with Jerry."

After the break, Red and Dusty walked to the forklift. Dusty sat in it and gave a sigh of relief. "It sure feels great to be back in this."

He leaned forward to turn the key in the ignition.

"What exactly do you think you're doing?" Jerry yelled from across the warehouse.

After a day of scrubbing toilets and two days of mopping, Dusty had just about had enough of Jerry. "I'm getting back to my job!"

"Think again, you little weasel. If you're finished sweeping the floor, you can start mopping it."

"What exactly is your problem?" Dusty fired back. "Didn't you hear your boss say that no one was pointing fingers about the missing guitar? Yet here you are pointing fingers at me!"

Jerry spoke in a low, menacing voice. "If you want to have a job here tomorrow, you'll get off that forklift and start pushing a mop around this place."

Red gave Dusty an understanding half-smile and then headed towards the loading dock.

Dusty got wearily off the forklift. "Where do I find the mop?" he asked, sounding resigned.

Jerry smirked at him. "Storage room by the employee bathroom."

• • •

Later in the day, Dusty sat at his usual booth in the diner. Cindy had been busy with other customers but brought some coffee which he sipped slowly since it was still very hot.

When the restaurant slowed down, Cindy headed over and plopped down beside him.

"You look really tired," she said after studying him for a moment.

"Yeah, I feel tired. I've been sweeping and now mopping the warehouse for three days straight. My feet ache."

"I'll bet. But why are you doing that job? I thought you were being paid to run the forklift."

"Well, ever since the guitar went missing Jerry has been riding me hard. First he made me clean the bathrooms, then sweep the floor. Now I'm mopping it. The good news is that I should finish the mopping tomorrow."

"So the guitar went missing three days ago?"

"That's right."

"Seems like Jerry is punishing you because it went missing."

"Seems that way, doesn't it."

"That's it!" Cindy banged her fist on the table, making Dusty's coffee cup jump slightly. She looked mad. "This has gone on long enough. Don't try to talk me out of it. I'm calling my father and putting a stop to this."

Dusty was too tired to argue. He just shrugged noncommittally. "Whatever you think is best. I just want to go home and sleep."

"I'll drive you back during my next break." She laid her hand on his and looked into his eyes. "I hope you know that the reason I'm going to call my father is that I'm concerned about you. What Jerry's doing to you is just plain wrong. I don't know what's gotten into him lately..."

• • •

Dusty felt a bit stiff the next day from all the manual labor. And he didn't know if Cindy had gotten a chance to talk to her father, but there was no sign of Tony at the warehouse.

He had found himself hoping Tony would show up in the morning and put an end to his mopping. But no such luck.

On the bright side, Dusty thought, *at least I'm almost done. Another half-hour should do it.*

When he finally finished mopping, Dusty headed back to the storage room next to the employee restroom to put the mop and pail away. As he came out of the storage room, Red was walking down the hall towards him.

"Everyone's in Jerry's office and you're wanted there too," Red said.

"Me?"

He followed Red to the office and found Jerry sitting behind his desk. Tim and Warren were gathered, and there was Tony. Everyone faced Jerry.

Dusty and Red squeezed around the sides of the desk.

"Now that everyone is here, we can start this little session," Tony began. "Seems after our last meeting, Jerry has been punishing Dusty." The boss turned to Jerry. "Were you unclear about what I meant when I said no one was pointing fingers, Jerry? What has gotten into you?"

"I really needed someone to sweep and mop the floors since Tim and Warren didn't have time the past several days."

"Why didn't you do it then?" Dusty asked hotly.

"Boys, is that true?" Tony asked, turning to the two pickers. "Did you not have time to do the sweeping and mopping?"

"No, sir," Warren said.

Tim shrugged. "Jerry told us not to do it."

Tony raised an eyebrow at Jerry. "Care to explain?"

Jerry opened his mouth, then closed it as if at a loss for what to say. Dusty watched Jerry's expression closely. The man's eyes went wide and the color drained from his face while suddenly staring fixedly at the doorway.

Dusty turned to see a teen boy standing there, holding a guitar case.

"Uh, Dad," the boy began, holding up the guitar case. He was looking right at Jerry when he said it. Was this Jerry's son? "Mom said I was to return this to you today."

Tony turned towards the door. "Hello, Adam. I'll take that. Thank you for bringing it by. You can go home now and let your mom know that you returned it. That's right."

The boss took the case and the teenager, Adam, turned to go.

When Dusty was sure the teenager was gone, he physically leaped on Jerry. He began to throttle him.

"You big fat jerk!" Dusty said, raising his voice. "You took the guitar and then made me clean those filthy bathrooms after you clogged them up! But that wasn't enough, was it? No! Then you made me sweep the whole warehouse and then mop it. It took me four days, you ugly brute. Four days!"

Dusty shook with fury, getting out all the emotion that had been pent up for the past four days. He felt hot and his hands were slick with sweat.

Jerry fought back and tried to break Dusty's hold. So far the anger had given Dusty enough strength to keep his hands around the man's neck, but he was starting to lose his grip.

That's when Tony and Red pulled him off Jerry.

"He's not worth it, Dusty," Red said.

Tony gave Jerry a hard look. "You make me sick. You're fired!"

Dusty stared at Tony, aghast. "You can't just fire him, not after what he did to me. He was the culprit all along! That guitar is worth a lot of money, isn't it? Can't you press charges, maybe talk a judge into giving him community work? Preferably doing something he hates, like maybe cleaning toilets or something."

Tony looked intently at Dusty. "You have a point there, son. Red, get the police on the horn. Tell them we have a thief here."

"No, not the police, Tony!" Jerry raised his hands in surrender. "Please, anything but that!"

Red's hand was on the desk phone. He looked at Tony for confirmation.

Tony nodded.

"With pleasure, sir!" Red picked up the phone and made the call.

Jerry looked trapped and kept touching his tongue to his dry lips. Trapped and guilty. He eyed the door and seemed to be wondering if he could escape.

But there were just too many people between him and freedom.

CHAPTER
THIRTY-EIGHT

DUSTY STOOD BY THE OUTER door and watched Jerry being led out of the warehouse in handcuffs and stuffed Into the back ot a police cruiser parked near the door. He noticed Inspector Baxter standing nearby with a cup of coffee in hand.

"Have you found my friends yet?" Dusty asked. "Charlie and Tina?"

Baxter looked up as if he had been deep in thought. His gaze sharpened. "We're working on it, Dusty."

Dusty lost it. Perhaps it was all the stress Jerry had been putting him through, or maybe it was seeing the inspector always drinking coffee and never doing anything, but Dusty had run out of patience.

"If you were as focused on finding my friends as you are in getting your regular dose of caffeine, you would have found them by now," he said accusingly. "You suck on that coffee like it's a soother. As if it was the most important thing to you!"

Spent, Dusty sank to the ground and sat there looking dejected.

Inspector Baxter looked down at his coffee cup. "Sorry, this coffee is just so good when they get the right mix of cream and sugar..."

"We're ready to go sir," an officer called out.

The inspector nodded and headed toward the cruiser. Just before getting in the car, he turned back to Dusty.

"Try to relax and leave this to us," Baxter assured him. "We have a vested interest in catching these bank robbers. And when we do, we'll find your friends. You can count on it."

With that, the inspector stepped into the cruiser. Soon it was moving off in the direction of the police station.

Dusty got up wearily and headed back into the warehouse where he saw the gang standing around Tony.

"So I think we'll shut down early today," Tony was saying. "You can all go home and we'll regroup tomorrow and figure out what to do about Jerry's position. But for now, I'll pay you for the day. You boys go and relax. Does that sound okay to everyone?"

Tim and Warren high-fived each other with a whoop. Red just nodded and Dusty nodded, too.

Dusty was heading back outside when Red caught up to him. "Need a ride?"

"Nah. I think I'll just walk, but thanks."

"Have you forgotten that we were shot at when we were at the bog?"

"No... no, I haven't forgotten," Dusty said. "I just need some fresh air, you know? A chance to stretch my legs. I'm sick of being driven everywhere the past three days!"

"What about the woman from the hotel who picks you up? Won't she be expecting to find you here when she comes?"

He hesitated. "You're right. I'll call her when I get to the diner."

"Why not call her now?" Red asked. "You can use Jerry's office."

Dusty looked at Red, then couldn't help it. He burst out laughing. He didn't really know why it was so funny; it was probably just another release of pent-up emotion after what Jerry had put him through.

When he started laughing, Red got a goofy grin on his face, which only made Dusty laugh all the more.

"Thanks," Dusty said when he recovered. "I needed that. It's been a brutal few days. But anyway, Wendy won't be here for a couple hours yet. Even if I can't use the phone at the diner, I'm sure Cindy could make the call for me."

"Fair enough, but I'm still concerned about you walking alone. What if people with guns start shooting at you again? Tell you what: I'll trail you slowly in my car, and if anything happens you can jump in and we'll peel out of there together."

Dusty realized that he was quite serious. "Sure. If it'll make you feel better. Why not."

He stuffed his hands in his jean pockets and started walking. A moment later, he heard Red's car start up and keep pace just behind him. His friend followed him all the way to the diner.

When Dusty entered, Cindy was by the counter cleaning up dirty dishes. She looked up.

"Dusty!" She came from around the counter and gave him a big hug. Breaking the hug, she rested her hands on Dusty's shoulders and looked him in the eye. "I heard from my dad that he showed up at the warehouse and Jerry was arrested. He's the one who took the guitar?"

Dusty nodded. "Yeah, I guess he took it home to show to his son."

"Adam?"

"I think that was his name. He brought it back today while your dad was there. Right when Jerry was trying to deny everything."

"Oh my goodness. Adam will be so devastated!"

"It's not his fault," Dusty said. "He was just being a good kid and bringing it back like his mom told him to."

"I know Adam. He'll feel as if he's the reason his dad is going to prison."

"Your dad hopes the judge will give him community service."

Just then, the bell over the door tinkled. They both turned in time to see an older man walk through the door. In came none other than Crackers, in the flesh.

Dusty was about to lunge towards him, but Cindy grabbed his arm and pulled him back.

"Now there, no reason to get hostile," Crackers said, grinning. "I only came in here to have some coffee."

"You think sending your goons to shoot us at Floggin's Bog is no reason to get hostile?" Dusty asked, seething.

"In all fairness, they were acting on their own. I've already bawled them out for it. It won't happen again. At least not from those two. You have my word on that."

Dusty rolled his eyes. "Big deal. You'll just send other goons in their place."

"No other goons. Just me."

"Is that a threat?" Dusty turned to Cindy. "Did you hear that? He just threatened me. Where are the coffee-drinking police when you need them?"

He looked wistfully around the practically empty diner.

When he turned back to Crackers, the man was just taking a seat at the front counter. He had his back to them. Dusty couldn't believe the audacity of the man.

"Could I could get some coffee?" Crackers asked.

CHAPTER
THIRTY-NINE

AFTER CRACKERS LEFT, DUSTY AND Cindy sat in their usual booth in the back of the restaurant and discussed what Crackers had said.

"Do you think he was serious when he said his people wouldn't come after you again?" Cindy asked.

"I'd like to think so. It would be nice not to need rides everywhere. I could become a bit more self-sufficient." Dusty snapped his fingers. "I forgot to call Wendy at the hotel! What time is it?"

"It's 12:30."

"I know I'm not allowed to use the phone here, but I need to call Wendy before she leaves to pick me up at the warehouse. Is there any chance I could use the phone?"

"I don't think Gus will mind this one time," she said. "There's one in the back. I'll show you."

Dusty followed her back into the kitchen, then into a small office off to the side from where Gus was standing behind the grill.

"Thanks for calling and letting me know, Dusty," Wendy said when Dusty got her on the line. "But where are you now and how are you going to get back here?"

"I'm at the diner and I'm just going to walk today."

"But that's not safe! Tell me what time you want me to come pick you up."

"It's not necessary," he insisted. "I already walked here from the warehouse. Also, Crackers showed up and said his people won't be bothering me anymore."

"And you trust him? You really trust that you'll be safe? Let me pick you up anyway, Dusty. It would make Tom and I feel better."

"I appreciate it, Wendy, but the truth is I'm sick of getting chauffeured everywhere I go. I just want to be free to walk where I want to go on my own schedule."

There was silence on the other end of the line.

"Hello?" Dusty said. "Are you still there, Wendy?"

"Yes, I'm still here. I've just been thinking. I understand how you feel, but do me a favor. If you change your mind about a ride, will you call me back?"

"Okay, yes. If I change my mind and Cindy doesn't force me into her car and drive me, I'll call you. I promise."

"Thank you, Dusty."

Dusty could hear real relief in her voice, and he hung up feeling puzzled.

When he came back to the front counter, a few new customers had shown up and Cindy was busy serving them. She signaled for Dusty to go find a seat in the back.

A few minutes later, Cindy showed up with some ice water and joined him at the table. "You look perplexed," she said.

"I don't really know how to explain it."

"Just start from the beginning."

"Well, ever since I showed up in town, Tom and Wendy at the hotel have been nothing but kind and helpful. I really like them... and I know they're super friendly. I just didn't realize they cared so much about me."

"So what happened to make you realize how much they care?"

"It was her voice on the phone. She sounded genuinely concerned for my safely. When I told her I wanted to walk back to the hotel, she said I should call her if I changed my mind. You should have heard the relief in her voice, Cindy. She'd have to be a very good actor to fake that."

"Maybe they just like you and want to help because you lost your friends. There's nothing wrong with that."

Dusty smiled at her. "You're right. That's what I like about you, Cindy. You have such a positive outlook on life."

Cindy took his hand in hers. "That's the nicest thing you've said to me." Then she leaned forward and gave him a light kiss. She grinned. "But I come by my positive outlook on life honestly. It's how I was raised."

Dusty just sat there feeling stunned, a goofy look on his face.

Cindy had to get up a couple times to serve customers. But when things quieted down, she dropped back into her seat at Dusty's table.

"Have you snapped out of your daze?" Cindy asked.

"Yeah, I think so. So, a question for you: how did your parents raise you to be such a positive person?"

"I think it's because they were so positive. And church helped."

"Church? I didn't know you ever went. Why didn't you tell me this before?"

"That's easy. You never asked. But it reminds me... Mrs. Wilcox invited us to her church and we haven't gone yet."

"True. We did say we'd go. How often do you go to church?"

"I used to go with my mom and dad, but since I've been living on my own I haven't been there lately," she said. "I guess it's easier to go when you're in a household where others are up early. It's not as easy when you live alone. But maybe we could go this Sunday?"

"Together?" Dusty asked.

"Of course!"

"Deal."

A short time later, Dusty headed back to the hotel on foot. He arrived unscathed and headed to his room, but only after checking in at the front desk to let Tom and Wendy know he was all right.

• • •

After work the next day, Dusty came back to the hotel to learn that he had a message waiting for him. Wendy told him that he was to call Inspector Baxter.

They've found Charlie and Tina! he thought.

"No, not yet," Baxter said when Dusty got him on the line. "I heard from the casino, whose money you located, and they say they owe you a half-million dollars as a reward for finding it. They want to know in what form you'd like the payment."

"Half a million?" Dusty said.

"Yes. Ten percent of the five million recovered."

The inspector then gave Dusty the phone number to call. "The person who called me from the casino seemed quite eager to get this taken care of. If I were you, I'd call them immediately."

After Dusty hung up, he called the casino.

"Hi, this is Dusty Burns—"

Before he could say more, the person on the other end of the line cut him off. It was a man's voice with a hearty boom to it. "Dusty Burns! We have a good chunk of money to give you. Our way of saying thank you for finding our money."

"So what do you need from me?" Dusty asked.

"We'd just like to know how you'd like the money delivered. Cash? Check? Money order?"

"And when exactly would you like to know this by?"

"Hmm. We'd like to get this settled as soon as possible, but we can give you a few days. Tell you what... today's Thursday, so how about you take the weekend and let us know Monday? Fair enough?"

Dusty agreed to call the man back Monday after explaining it likely wouldn't happen until after work in the afternoon.

"No problem," the man said.

CHAPTER
FORTY

"HALF A MILLION DOLLARS!" CINDY squealed as Dusty sat at his usual table and told her the news that evening. "I mean, I know the newspaper said you'd get ten percent, but it seems so much more real now that you've talked to the casino."

"Shhh, not so loud. But yes. I just have to think how I'd like to get it. You know, cash or check."

"Cash, of course."

"It's not that simple. If I take cash and return home to pay off the loan shark, he's the sort of person who'll just take all my money and leave me with nothing.

Cindy's face fell. "I see what you mean. So what are you going to do?"

"I don't know yet. I'm hoping an idea will come to me before Monday."

"Oh, that reminds me. I bumped into Mrs. Wilcox this morning and told her we'd go to church with her on Sunday."

Dusty made eye contact. "Where is this church?"

"It's not far. I'll meet you here at the diner at about 9:45 and we can walk over together. Church starts at 10:00."

"Sounds like a plan." But his mind wasn't really on church. "I just can't stop thinking about how to handle this money and get the Grub off my back forever. First I need to get the money without Crackers hearing about it. He'll think it belongs to him. You won't tell anyone, will you? I mean, other than all the people in here who heard you scream out the amount?"

Cindy's hand flew to her mouth. "Oh gosh, I'm so sorry about that, Dusty." She took a look around, but there were only two customers and they were near the front. "I hope they just didn't pay any attention to what I said. Mr. Thompson is half deaf, so I doubt he heard." She gnawed on her fingernail. "I'll never forgive myself if you lose this money because of my big mouth."

Dusty touched her arm. "Let's not worry about it. What's done is done. Now, when I get this reward money I'll need to head back to Edmonton to pay back the loan shark."

Cindy looked up at him, studying his face. "Y–you're leaving then?" A few tears rolled down her cheeks.

"Just temporarily. I actually hope to come back once that's done, once things are safe for us again. Then maybe we could go to Alberta together? You know, so I can introduce you to my family?"

Cindy took his hand and squeezed it. "Of course I will."

Dusty smiled. "Even after I pay off the loan shark, I'll still need to find Charlie and Tina and get Crackers and his gang off my back. Only then will things be safe."

New customers arrived and Cindy ran off to serve them.

CHAPTER
FORTY-ONE

THE NEXT MORNING, DUSTY WAS still enjoying the fact that Jerry was gone. All the stress and strain of the job had rolled away and he felt like a great weight had been lifted off his shoulders. He no longer had to even think about cleaning restrooms or mopping floors. Besides, Tim and Warren had a good system for getting the floors done in no time at all.

Without any worries at work, the day went by quickly and before Dusty knew it lunch had arrived. He sat with Red, as had become his routine, and told him about the reward money.

"I was with you," Red remarked. "Shouldn't I get a part of that?"

"Ah. Yes, of course. When I was finding the money, what were you doing again? Oh right, using the men's room."

"But I was still there. And remember? I helped you get out!"

Dusty thought back, recalling that he'd suddenly felt weak when they had heard someone coming. "You're right. How much would you like?"

"I'm not a greedy man. Besides, I consider you a friend. How about twenty thousand?"

Dusty raised his eyebrows at this. "I have to pay back the loan shark before I can commit to any amount. I don't even know how much I'll have left. But I'll do what I can. Is that good enough for you?"

Red grinned. "Of course. I trust you, Dusty. Ever since you pulled me out of the bog, I knew you were trustworthy. Twenty thousand would help me get some things taken care of and maybe get a newer car. But whatever you can do, I'll be happy with that. And that's because I know you aren't cheap and won't send me just one dollar."

They shook hands and then went back to work.

• • •

Sunday came bright and early. Dusty walked over to meet Cindy, and as he approached the diner he saw her sitting on the front steps.

She got to her feet. "You're looking good, Dusty."

"Well, so are you. You look very nice in that dress."

She wore a light-colored summer dress with pastel yellows and pinks. Dusty had worn black dress pants and black dress shoes with a simple button-up white shirt with collar. It was too warm out for a jacket.

As Cindy had promised, it was a short walk to church, where Mrs. Wilcox met them in the entryway.

"I'm so glad you both could make it," the older woman said, beaming.

"Thank you for inviting us," Cindy replied. "It's been ages since I was in church."

Mrs. Wilcox patted her hand. "Let's go find a seat before they fill up."

She led them to seats at the front, and all the while people Dusty had never met came up, shook his hand, and welcomed him. The amazing thing was, they all seemed to genuinely mean it. He found it all a bit overwhelming. He'd never experienced anything quite like it.

They sat in the padded chairs placed side by side, all in a row. Dusty sat in the middle with Cindy on his right and Mrs. Wilcox on his left.

The service started off with announcements, which Dusty largely ignored since they didn't pertain to him. Then a few people came onto the stage. One had a guitar while another sat at the piano. Two were singers, and together the group led the congregation in some songs. Dusty got swept up in the music and felt a warmth surround him.

Suddenly, he saw clear as day what to do with the half-million-dollar reward. The revelation was so unexpected and real that Dusty sank to his knees, overcome with emotion.

During the sermon, he was so lost in what he'd just seen and experienced that he lost track of time. Only a minute after the preaching seemed to have started, the service came to a sudden end. The people around him were getting up to leave.

Mrs. Wilcox turned to Dusty. "Are you okay? What happened to you during the service?"

Dusty cleared his throat. "I'm not sure if I can explain it."

"Just try," Cindy said. "Come on, Dusty, you can do this."

He felt Cindy slip her hand into his, encouraging him to go on. "Well, I felt this warmth envelop me during the singing and I fell to my knees. It was incredible, but I can't really explain what happened."

"That was Jesus," Mrs. Wilcox said.

"I also saw very clearly what to do with the money... how much to get in cash and how much to get in a different form."

Mrs. Wilcox looked baffled.

"Did you see the paper a few days ago that said Dusty was getting a reward for finding that bank heist money?" Cindy asked.

"Oh yes, of course."

"I have to pay back a loan shark back home," Dusty explained. "I didn't know how to break the money up so the loan shark would be happy, but now I know."

"So what did you see?" Cindy asked.

"I'll take a hundred thousand dollars in cash and the rest in a cashier's check. I'll bring the cash with me to the loan shark, keeping the cashier's check for myself. I have a feeling the loan shark will take all the cash, even though it's twice as much as what I owe him. He'll probably say it's interest. But at least it will get him out of my life for good." He paused for a moment. "There's a little more to the plan I saw, but that's all I can say for now."

Mrs. Wilcox put her hand on Dusty's knee. "God wants the best for you. If you just follow His advice, it will all work out."

CHAPTER
FORTY-TWO

AFTER CHURCH, DUSTY AND CINDY said goodbye to Mrs. Wilcox and thanked her for inviting them. They headed off on foot.

"Are you hungry?" Dusty asked as they walked along.

"I'm surprised you need to ask," Cindy said. "Didn't you hear my stomach in church?"

"Can't say I did. But then, maybe the noise my stomach made drowned it out."

She caught Dusty by the hand and sped up. "Then let's find somewhere to eat. Somewhere other than the diner!"

They found a little restaurant not far from the diner. But nothing in town was far from it.

When they were seated and had ordered, Cindy leaned back with a contented sigh. "So were you serious about having me join you back in Edmonton to meet your family?"

"Of course. But I'll need to go back as soon as I collect the reward money. It wouldn't do to have a hundred thousand dollars in cash here for long. Otherwise Crackers and his gang will hear about it, I'm sure. Word seems to spread fast in a small town. Then they'll try to steal it from me. No. The best bet is to leave as soon as I get it."

"But how will you get home?"

"I was going to ask Red if he'd give me a lift to the train station in Saskatoon. I'll book a return ticket once I pay off the Grub. Then we can go meet my family together... whenever it works."

"I'm rather glad you don't want me to come meet him, too." Cindy giggled. "Oh, and if Red can't drive you, I will."

Dusty smiled. "That's very kind of you."

• • •

Work went by quickly the following day as Dusty loaded flats into waiting trucks. Afterward he had lunch with Red.

"So you have to phone the casino back today?" Red asked.

"Yeah, right after work. I wonder if they'll bring the money here or if I'll have to go there to get it?"

"I guess you'll find out soon enough, buddy." Red grinned and slapped him on the shoulder. "What town is this casino in again?"

"Trimble. How far a drive is that?"

"About four hours."

"Hmm. Well, I guess you're right, I'll find out soon enough. No sense worrying about it now. Let's go back to work and get everything done."

"You got it," Red replied.

When Dusty returned to the hotel after work, he flopped onto the bed and grabbed the phone on the nightstand. He dialed the number of the casino, then brought the receiver to his ear.

"So what have you decided, young man?" the man asked in his booming voice.

"Well, sir, I'd really like one hundred thousand in cash, one check made out to someone else, and the remainder in a cashier's check made out to me. Is that possible?"

"Of course! Anything is possible. Now, are you sure you don't want it all in cash? You could come try your luck at our casino…"

"Uh, no thank you," Dusty mumbled. He hoped the fellow was just yanking his chain.

The man laughed uproariously. "I don't blame you, young fellow, not one bit."

Dusty gave the name and amount he wanted on the check. "So how do I, uh, get this money? You can't exactly mail me one hundred thousand dollars in cash."

The man laughed again. "You're so right. Well, as it happens, I'll be heading your way tomorrow. Business in the area. So we can meet up. I'll give you the money just the way you requested."

"Perfect," Dusty said. "When and where?"

"Anywhere you choose."

"All right. There's a restaurant here in town called the First Street Diner."

"I assume it's on First Street?"

"Actually, no. It moved at some point but apparently kept the name. It's on Fifth Street, just off Main."

The man paused, perhaps to write down the name of the street. "I'll find it. Now, I know you work in the mornings, but what time works for you in the afternoon?"

"I'm usually done by one o'clock. We could meet at, say, two o'clock? That will give me a bit of leeway if work runs a few minutes long."

"Two o'clock it is. See you then."

And the man hung up.

After putting down the phone, Dusty wandered out to the front desk to talk to Tom or Wendy, who both happened to be there.

"Dusty!" they said in unison.

"What can we do for you?" Wendy asked.

"I'd like to pay my bill."

She looked at him sadly. "You're leaving?"

"No, not yet. I just want to pay what I've racked up on credit." Dusty took a wad of money from his pocket. "How much do I owe?"

Tom looked at the computer and tapped a few keys. "For your room and the meals you put on credit in the past three weeks, it comes to seventeen hundred dollars."

Dusty peeled off two thousand dollars and handed it over, placing the remaining cash in his pocket. "That will cover it plus a bit extra to account for any incidentals during the rest of my stay—that is, until I find my friends. If I owe any after, I'll settle then."

"Sounds fair," Tom said. "Just out of curiosity, do you aways carry thousands of dollars around in your pocket?"

"Not usually." Dusty grinned. "The pay at the warehouse is really good, so I've been able to save lots. But this brings me to the other reason I wanted to talk." He went on to explain the reward money he was about to receive. "I want to lock up the cash safe and sound so

I can take it with me as soon as I'm ready to return home to pay off the loan shark. But I don't want to leave it in my hotel room. Is there somewhere around here I could rent a locker? Like at a bus station?"

"We can do better than that," Tom told him. "We have an old safe in the back that will handle a large bag of money. We can keep it secure for you until you need it."

Dusty studied them closely, not sure whether he could trust them with that much money.

As if seeing the uncertainty in his eyes, Tom added, "We like you, Dusty. That's why we covered your food and hotel bills until you were in a position to pay us back."

"Here's the truth," Wendy said. "We never had children of our own, and we just took a real shine to you when you first showed up. We wanted to help in any way we could."

Dusty felt a lump form in his throat. Other than Charlie and Tina, and now Cindy and Red, had he ever felt that anyone really cared about his well-being?

He turned away so they wouldn't see the moisture in his eyes. "Thanks. I'll bring it by tomorrow afternoon."

"Do you want one or both of us to come with you to this meeting tomorrow?" Tom asked. "You know, for moral support. Then we can drive you and the money back here. It would be a lot safer than walking over with a big bag of cash."

Dusty wiped the tears from his eyes by pinching the bridge of his nose. He turned back around to face them. "That would be great! I'm supposed to meet the man from the casino at two o'clock at the diner where Cindy works."

"We'll be there," Wendy said.

Dusty felt the sudden urge to hug them both, but instead he thanked them and headed to his room. On the way, he shook himself.

What's wrong with me? he wondered. *Almost crying in front of Tom and Wendy and then having an incredible urge to hug them both for being so helpful... maybe I'm just overtired. What I need is a good long sleep tonight.*

CHAPTER
FORTY-THREE

AT LUNCH, DUSTY TOLD RED about his meeting with the casino representative after work.

"Would you give me a ride to the diner to get my reward money?" he asked.

"You mean *our* money, don't you?"

Dusty ran his hand nervously through his hair. "Uh… I guess so."

Red laughed and banged the table in his mirth. "I'm just yanking your chain. Of course I'll give you a ride. I can drive you to the hotel afterward, too, if you'd like."

"That's okay. Tom and Wendy are meeting me, so that's covered. And thanks."

The rest of the shift went by quickly. Dusty loaded two trucks with full pallets and then the work was done.

"Just let me do a bit of paperwork and then we can head off," Red said as he walked to the back where he now occupied Jerry's old office.

Dusty sat on the floor of the big warehouse and leaned against the wall. He thought about Cindy and what a delight she was, how they had forged a strong bond in such a short time. He'd become good friends with her, and he felt that it had blossomed into something more.

He also thought of the others in town who had turned out to be good friends, like Red and Tom and Wendy. He had never found people who took to him so quickly. It touched him deeply.

But he still needed to find Charlie and Tina. He missed their friendship too.

He let out a sigh.

"Why the big sigh?" Red asked.

Dusty jumped, not having heard Red come back. "Just reminiscing."

"Still haven't found your two friends, have we?"

"No. But I'm hopeful we will soon. Anyway, I don't miss them as much as I would have if I hadn't had you and Cindy in my life."

"Let's get going before you have me weeping," Red said with a big grin. "Besides, we don't want to be late to get our money."

Dusty laughed. "You're right. Let's get going then, shall we?"

When they arrived at the diner, Dusty got out of the car.

"Want me to come in and meet this guy with you?" Red asked.

"I'm okay. Cindy and the cook are here, plus Tom and Wendy will be showing up right away. This guy from the casino isn't going to steal from me... he could have done that without coming here."

"When you're right, you're right," Red said. "See you at work tomorrow, bud."

"You bet!"

Dusty went inside. Cindy waved when he walked in the door.

He looked around but didn't see any new faces. The man from the casino obviously hadn't arrived yet. He went to his usual booth in the back and waited.

He didn't have to wait long. Within minutes, a portly man in a suit bustled into the diner with a briefcase clutched in his right hand. He looked around, and when Dusty stood up the man headed towards him.

"Dusty Burns?"

"The one and the same." Dusty noticed that the man's suit was rumpled, and his dark hair looked as if he had just run his fingers through it. He was a bit shorter than Dusty but had broad shoulders which made him look a little taller than he actually was. All in all, he had the look of a busy, harried man.

Dusty took a seat and waved to the seat opposite him.

Once the man in the suit had removed his jacket and opened his briefcase, he removed a business card and handed it to Dusty.

Jerrod Mueller, Accounts Manager
Tumbleweed Casino
Trimble, Saskatchewan

Dusty read the card and then raised his eyes to meet Jerrod's.

"Do you have any identification on you?" Jerrod asked.

"Of course." Dusty pulled out his wallet, removed the driver's license, and handed it to the man.

Jerrod looked from the picture to Dusty a few times, then read the particulars before handing it back. "We have to make sure we're giving money to the correct person. You understand."

"Of course."

Jerrod opened his briefcase again, removed a simple white envelope, and handed it to Dusty. "The cash is in my car. If you'll come with me, I'll give it you."

Dusty slid the envelope into his back pocket and then followed the man outside. Jerrod's car was parked right in front.

Dusty looked around but didn't spot anyone else around. Jerrod popped the trunk and pulled out a medium-sized duffel bag and handed it to Dusty. It was heavier than Dusty expected.

"Twenties, nonsequential bills, and that should conclude our transaction," Jerrod said. "Let's go back in."

Back at the table, Jerrod opened his briefcase again and pulled out a form.

"I just need you to sign this to say you received the money."

"Shouldn't I check to see if it's all here?" Dusty asked.

Jerrod sat down and stared complacently at Dusty. "By all means."

Dusty pulled the envelope from his back pocket, slid the unsealed top open, and removed both a cashier's check and personal check made out just the way he had requested. He returned them to the envelope and then put it back in his pocket.

He picked up the duffel from the floor where he had set it and hoisted it onto the table. He zipped it open and saw neat bundles of twenty-dollar bills. He rifled through them a bit, but it all looked aboveboard.

"You're sure the correct amount's in here?"

"Quite sure." Jerrod looked amused. "Look, Mr. Burns…"

"Please, just Dusty. Mr. Burns is my father."

Jerrod nodded. "Of course. Like I was about to say, if I'd wanted to procure any of this for myself, I would not have shown up here today."

The man handed him three pages of paperwork, along with a pen. He then showed Dusty where to sign the form in triplicate.

Once the forms were signed, Jerrod gave Dusty a copy and put the other two copies in his briefcase, which he snapped closed.

He donned his jacket and held out a hand. Dusty shook it.

"It's been a pleasure, Dusty. Now, I have another appointment soon, so I bid you a fond farewell."

Dusty raised his hand in farewell as Jerrod departed the diner.

When he had left, Cindy came over and gave him a hug.

"How does it feel to be rich?" she asked mischievously.

"I'm far from rich." He grinned. "But it feels great!" Then Dusty became serious. "I need to ask you a favor, Cindy."

They sat down and Dusty pulled out the envelope. He removed the cashier's check and gave the envelope to Cindy.

"Once I'm headed back to Edmonton, would you see that Red gets this?" he asked. "It's a big thank you for all the help he's been. Did I ever tell you about the day I found the bank heist money?"

Cindy shook her head and leaned forward as Dusty told her the entire story.

"When I found the money, Red had gone to use the restroom," he said at the end of it. "That's when we heard someone else coming, and my legs turned to jelly. I didn't have the strength to get out of there. If Red hadn't physically helped me, who knows what might have happened? I might have disappeared like my friends."

When Tom and Wendy showed up, they took Dusty and his money back to the hotel. Dusty watched as Tom opened the safe and put the duffel with the money inside. He then closed it and spun the dial.

"There, it's secure," Tom said, patting the top of the safe with his hand. "This safe is built like a tank. It might be old, but it's sturdy and reliable. Plus it's bolted to the floor so thieves can't take just pick it up and carry it out of here. Not that they'd have an easy time of that. This baby weighs over four hundred pounds."

CHAPTER
FORTY-FOUR

DUSTY DROVE THE FORKLIFT AT work but couldn't get his mind off the money and what it would mean to pay off the Grub and be free of him and his goons forever. That and the fact that after he gave some money to Red, something to really help his friend out, he'd have plenty left over. What would he do with that much money? Maybe he could use it to buy a house for him and Cindy. That is, if she'd have him.

Before he knew it his break had arrived. He and Red sat together in the break room.

"So have you given any thought to what you'll do with the reward money?" Red asked.

"As a matter of fact, I have. I have an idea or two kicking around."

"Care to share?"

"At this point it's just conjecture and nothing exciting... like buying a yacht or an airplane. But speaking of the money, I have to go back to Edmonton to pay off that loan shark. Only when that's done can I really put this behind me."

Red nodded. "So what are you thinking? Driving there?"

"Actually, I was thinking of taking the train and hopefully arriving unnoticed."

"The train? You'll need to get to Saskatoon to catch it."

"That's right. You feel like giving me a lift?"

"No can do, buddy," Red said. "I'd like to, don't get me wrong, but my mom fell down the stairs two days ago and broke both her ankles. I've been spending all my spare time looking after her. Except for work. I can't be away from her too long in case she needs help. A neighbor lady looks after her while I'm at work, but she has her own family to take care of. So I'm pretty much tied up after work."

"It's amazing she didn't break her neck," Dusty said. "You don't have any family to help you out?"

"My old man passed away a couple years ago and my only sibling lives in Toronto."

"Brother?"

"Sister."

"I'm sorry to hear about your mom, Red. I've been so caught up in my own life that I didn't even notice you were going through an ordeal. I'm sorry. And don't worry about me. I'll find some way to get to the train station."

"Thank you, buddy. I know you've had a lot going on. It's okay."

Later, when Dusty arrived at the diner, Cindy was behind the front counter serving people food and refilling drinks. She looked up as Dusty came in and gave him a big smile. She held up two fingers to say she'd be free in two minutes and gestured to the seating in the back.

Dusty headed there and took a seat in one of the booths.

Moments later, Cindy plopped down in the seat across from him, a huge smile on her face. It instantly put a smile on Dusty's face, too.

Cindy slid a coffee across to him, then lifted her own mug to her lips and sipped. With a sigh of contentment, she set it back on the table.

Dusty noted the angles of her jaw and marveled at how exquisite she looked. But it wasn't her looks that drew him to her; it was her personality, her wanting to help him any way she could, her thoughtfulness and kindness. He marveled at how easy it was to talk to her. Those were the qualities he found most attractive.

He thought of some advice his grandfather had once given him: "Never marry for looks, Dusty, but rather for who the person is on the inside. Looks will fade, but there's a good chance that the person they are inside will remain the same."

Dusty reached out and took Cindy's hands in his. "I have another favor to ask."

"Well, don't keep me in suspense. What is it you need from me?"

"Red can't drive me to the train station in Saskatoon, so are you still willing to take me?"

Cindy squeezed his hands. "Of course I'll take you. On one condition, though."

Dusty raised his eyebrows. "Yes?"

"That you come back here after you've paid back that loan shark."

He rubbed his thumb across Cindy's fingers. "Of course I will." He released one of her hands and took a sip of his coffee. Setting the coffee cup back on the table, he asked, "When do you think we can go? I really want to deal with this matter as soon as possible."

"I have some vacation time coming up. I just have to talk to Gus and nail down the dates. When you come by tomorrow—that is, if you can—I should know."

"Thanks, Cindy. That takes a load off my mind."

Dusty leaned forward, lifted her hand to his lips, and kissed it. Cindy beamed, her eyes sparkling.

CHAPTER
FORTY-FIVE

BACK AT THE HOTEL LATER that afternoon, Dusty thought about his Aunt Mae. Feeling inspired, he got up and headed to the main desk.

"Hi Wendy," Dusty said when Wendy looked up from some paperwork. "Is there by any chance a mailbox nearby?"

"Oh yes, there is. One block north of here."

"Perfect. I'd like to write a letter to my aunt. She hasn't heard from me in a while. Any idea where I can buy a postage stamp and an envelope, plus find a blank piece of paper?"

"That is so sweet of you, Dusty. I'm sure I have paper and an envelope I can scrounge up here. I have a few stamps that we keep on hand for guests. How many do you need?"

"Just one."

Dusty paid her for the stamp. Wendy threw in an envelope and single sheet of lined paper for free.

He went back to his room and wrote the letter. Sealing it in the envelope, he stuck the postage stamp on it. A few minutes later, he headed outside and walked a block north where he spied the red mailbox on the corner. He mailed his letter and then strolled back to the hotel, whistling softly to himself.

• • •

Work sped by the next day, with Dusty kept busy loading trucks right up until closing. Afterwards, as he walked to the diner, he fell deep into thought.

As he began to cross the street, he heard an engine rev.

He looked up just in time to see the grill of a pickup truck bearing down on him. He got only a quick glimpse of the driver, but clear as day he recognized Crackers behind the wheel with a look of pure maniacal delight on his face.

Dusty only had a couple of seconds to react, though it seemed much longer. He turned and leapt back onto the sidewalk, but in the process his leg crashed into the side of a fire hydrant, hitting just above the kneecap. Pain shot through his leg, and at the same time he felt relieved that he hadn't been run over.

As he lay on the sidewalk, he watched the pickup drive away.

Shaken, he lay his head on the pavement and let his heart calm down. When he sat up, he rolled his pantleg up and took a look at his knee. It looked pretty normal. He couldn't tell if it was swollen.

He touched it and found that the muscle above the knee was sore. He rolled his pantleg gingerly down and struggled to his feet. But it hurt to walk normally and his leg started to throb.

Just great.

He continued to the diner, but this time with a limp. When he finally arrived, Cindy took one look at him before rushing over and helping him over to a nearby table.

"What happened?" Cindy asked.

Dusty told her about the truck driver who had tried to run him over. "He came out of nowhere."

"And you're sure it was Crackers?"

"Positive. His death skull grin is a little hard to forget."

"Does it hurt much?"

"It's not bad," Dusty said. "Just a little sore. I banged it on a fire hydrant as I avoided being run over. I'm sure it will be fine."

She helped him get comfortable in the seat. "Can I get you anything? I have to keep working, as the afternoon crowd should be in soon. I have to change the coffee filters. Can I get you a fresh cup when that's done?"

"Actually, a cold glass of water would be great, thanks."

Cindy smiled at him and then went off to fetch him a water. When she returned, she had something wrapped in a tea towel in her other hand.

"I've got some ice for your knee, in case it's hurting."

With that, she bustled back to the front and got busy getting the restaurant ready for the afternoon crowd. In a few minutes, about a dozen people showed up. It was just enough to keep Cindy hopping.

Dusty watched her work while holding the ice on his left knee with one hand and occasionally sipping his glass of water with the other. All in all he had a pleasant afternoon.

He thought about calling Tony to let them know he'd likely be off work for a few days, not to mention the fact that he'd need to go to Edmonton to take care of a financial matter. Then he realized that it was Friday. Besides, with four hundred thousand dollars, he wouldn't need to work for a while. Not if he played it smart.

Instead he contemplating giving his notice.

Finally the afternoon crowd was gone and Cindy came over and sat in the seat opposite him.

"Whew, that was busy," she said. "My shift is over if you'd like a ride home."

"That would be nice."

"If you keep your leg iced until tomorrow afternoon, you should be mobile enough to go out. I'll pick you up after work and take you to the police station to file a report."

"Okay."

"Wait here. I'll get my car and bring it out front."

"I didn't know you had a car," Dusty said. "Last time you drove me, you used Gus's truck."

"That's only because I don't always have my car at work. Sometimes I walk. But today I needed my car to run an errand before my shift. So don't move until I get back. I'll help you out."

"I'm not an invalid."

Cindy rested her had on his arm. "I know. Just humor me." Then she jumped up and bounced out the door.

Two minutes later, Cindy was back to help Dusty out of the booth and make his way to the door and into her passenger seat.

Dusty relaxed and closed his eyes. By the time he opened them, he saw that Cindy had stopped the car at the drug store, just a few blocks away.

"I'll be right back," Cindy said. "I just want to find something to hold the ice on your knee while you sleep."

She popped out of the car and walked into the store. A few minutes later, she came back empty-handed.

"Didn't they have anything?" Dusty asked.

"Oh, they did. But the lady in there said you don't need to keep it iced all night. Just several times a day for fifteen to twenty minutes at a time. Do you have a fridge with a freezer in your room?"

"I have a minifridge, but the freezer is too small to hold much. Why?"

"One more stop then."

Dusty looked at her quizzically, but Cindy just smiled, buckled up, and drove a few more blocks. This time they stopped in the parking lot of the grocery store.

Cindy disappeared inside but came back just a moment later with a small bag in her hand.

"What's in there?" Dusty asked.

"It's a surprise," Cindy said brightly. She tossed the bag in the back seat.

After buckling up, she drove Dusty to the hotel. She helped him out of the car and he placed his arm around her shoulders.

When Tom and Wendy saw Dusty being helped into the hotel, they rushed over.

"What happened?" Wendy asked breathlessly. "Were you attacked? Tom, help him."

"It's nothing," Dusty said. "My leg is just a bit sore."

Tom grabbed ahold of Dusty from the other side and together he and Cindy assisted him to his room while Dusty hopped on his good leg. Wendy followed along behind.

They settled him in a chair beside the bed with a small table in front of him. Cindy helped him get comfortable.

Wendy waited until he was settled, then sat on the edge of the bed. "Out with it, Dusty. I'm dying to hear what happened."

Dusty told about his narrow escape from being mowed down by Crackers in a pickup truck.

"Do you know what type of truck it was?" Tom asked.

"Sure. It was a little hard to miss the emblem on the front of the truck as it was bearing down on me. Plus I saw it coming and going. It was a Dodge Ram, quad cab."

"Did you get the license?" Wendy asked, bouncing with excitement.

"Calm down, Wendy," Tom said. "I'm sure Dusty will tell us soon enough."

"Unfortunately, the license plate was mud-splattered. I didn't get much of a look at it anyway."

Wendy rose. "I'll ring the police for you and tell them what you just said. You just sit and relax."

"But I have a phone right here in the room."

"That's okay, dear," she said. "Let a lady have a bit of fun, will you? It's not every day I get to ring the police and tell them of a crime. Attempted murder at that!"

With that, Wendy swept out of the room, the door closing softly behind her.

CHAPTER
FORTY-SIX

WHEN WENDY LEFT, CINDY PICKED up the bag she'd bought at the grocery store and opened it.

"Here is your surprise Dusty!" She pulled out a hot/cold pack. "You can keep this in your freezer when you're not using it. It will be easier than constantly making ice cubes. Just be sure to wrap it in a towel so it's not so cold on your skin. At least that's what the pharmacist told me."

She leaned over and handed it to Dusty.

Before he could say anything, she removed a second item from the bag. "And this is a little treat for you." She handed him a chocolate bar, then reached for the hot/cold pack. "Do you want me to put that in the freezer for you?"

Dusty handed it over. "Yes, and thank you."

"Do you have a hand towel? You could use that to wrap the pack in once it's cold."

Tom, who had been sitting quietly on the bed, jumped up. "There should be extras in the bathroom. I'll check."

He walked over to the bathroom and disappeared inside. He returned a moment later with a folded white hand towel and set it on the table between Dusty and Cindy.

A few minutes later, Wendy knocked on the door and Tom let her in. Wendy entered looking flushed and more excited than Dusty had ever seen her.

"I called the police and spoke to Sergeant Larsen," she explained. "He said he's coming over right away to question you directly."

"Oh lovely," Dusty said. "My old buddy Squid Larsen."

Wendy looked surprised. "Squid?"

"Oh, that's a nickname he got in basic training. Some of the officers still call him that."

"That sounds cruel," Wendy remarked.

Tom shrugged.

Wendy looked at her watch as realization flooded her eyes. "Oh dear. He'll be here any second. I'd better go wait up front so I can bring him to your room as soon as he arrives."

"I'll go wait with her," Tom said.

The couple both got up and left the room, the door closing softly behind them.

Cindy smiled at Dusty. "I talked to Gus, and after this weekend I can drive you to Saskatoon to catch the train to Edmonton."

"So we can head to the train station on Monday?" Dusty asked.

"If you like. I have the whole week off, so whichever day works for you."

Just then, they heard a knock on the door. Cindy got up and answered it, letting in Sergeant Larsen and Inspector Baxter. Once she had opened the door Cindy came back to the table and sat down.

"Excuse me, miss," Larsen said. "Could we have a private word with Mr. Burns?"

Dusty looked at them with determination. "She stays."

"I beg your pardon?" Larsen asked.

"You heard me. She stays."

Baxter touched the sergeant on the shoulder. "It's okay, Ted. She can stay."

"Whatever you say," Larsen said as he pulled a notebook out of his jacket pocket.

Since both chairs at the table were taken, Baxter and Larsen took seats on the side of the bed and faced them.

"Now Dusty, can you tell us in your own words what happened tonight?" Baxter said.

While Dusty recounted his near-fatal experience, Larsen wrote down all the details in his notebook. When Dusty was finished and Larsen was done writing, he handed the notebook over to Dusty.

"If this is accurate, please sign the bottom," Larsen said, handing Dusty his pen.

Dusty read it over, deemed it accurate, and signed his name as instructed. He handed the book back to Larsen.

Both men then thanked him and headed for the door.

"Uh, Inspector, any news on my friends?" Dusty asked before they were gone.

Baxter turned back at the door to face him. "Not yet. But we're eliminating Crackers' houses one at a time. This is not a quick process. We only have a couple of men to put on this. The rest are needed to keep the peace on their regular patrols. Plus, new events keep happening, requiring us to pull the men off their search. So it's slow going."

"Well, I hope you find them soon."

"You and me both, Dusty. You and me both." The inspector pulled open the door and walked out.

Once the police had gone, Cindy turned to Dusty. "I better get running, too," she said. "I have a few things to do tonight at home. I'll call you tomorrow and see how you're doing."

"All right. Thanks for everything. Talk to you tomorrow."

Dusty hobbled to his feet and gave her a hug before collapsing back in his chair. Cindy got her purse and headed to the door. Before leaving, she turned and gave him a little wave and a smile. Then she was gone.

CHAPTER
FORTY-SEVEN

INSPECTOR BAXTER LEANED AGAINST THE wall and held the phone to his ear. All the phones were being used except the payphone in the hallway of the police station.

The same phone the prisoners use, he thought wryly.

There was no spare chair for Baxter to use, so he leaned against the cinder block wall, the cord keeping him on a very short leash. There were no prisoners currently, but Baxter could hear the sound of keys tapping, coffee mugs being placed back on desks, and a murmur of voices as the other officers did their work.

The phone on the other end started to ring.

"Hello," said the voice through the receiver. It was Sanderson "Hello, sir."

"Is that you, Baxter?" the superintendent asked.

"Yes, sir."

"So what have you learned up there in Duggan?"

"Just that you were right about that missing persons report being related to the bank heist money," Baxter said.

"How so, Inspector?"

"The man who filed the report is the same man who found the missing loot and turned it over to the police."

"Now that is very interesting."

"There's more, sir. Seems the bank robbers are the ones who kidnapped the missing friends."

Baxter shifted the phone to his other ear as two officers walked by in an animated discussion.

"Missing friends, Inspector?" the superintendent asked.

"Yes, sir. The man who found the money and filed the missing persons report, Dusty Burns, is looking for his two friends, who disappeared the night they arrived in Duggan. We firmly believe the robbers are the ones responsible for that."

The superintendent laughed. "I like it, Inspector. I really do. But what are you doing to locate this man's friends?"

"Well, sir, we're finding that the leader of the bank robbers has multiple homes, all listed in his ex-wife's name. Unfortunately we have limited resources up here."

"No luck so far, Inspector?"

"Not yet, sir, but we're only halfway through the properties in the two weeks we've been searching."

"Fill me in once you find them, won't you?"

Baxter shifted his position, aiming to get the kink out of his back. "Of course, sir."

"What other news do you have from Duggan, Inspector?"

"For starters, sir, the leader of robbers is known as Crackers."

"Crackers?"

"That's right, sir."

"It's not a name that would breed much confidence, now is it?"

"No, sir, it certainly isn't. But it probably helps keep his gang in check. As you likely know, sir, the word crackers means nuts... or crazy. Personally, I think 'certifiably insane' fits the bill better. From what I've heard."

"Any other news?"

"Dusty and two of his friends were shot at by Crackers's gang while walking in a local nature reserve."

"Crackers actually shot at Dusty Burns and two locals?"

"Two members of his gang did the shooting, sir."

"Keep an eye on this Dusty fellow, Inspector. I have a gut feeling Crackers is going to live up to his name soon."

"Roger that, sir."

For the second time during this call, the superintendent laughed. "It amuses me to no end to know that Dusty Burns found the stolen money and turned it in only because the bank robbers grabbed his two friends."

Sanderson was still laughing when Baxter hung up the payphone and walked away.

CRACKERS, AT HIS HOME OFFICE in one of his many houses, sat behind his desk and glared at Jackson, Vi, and Grimsby. "When are you three clowns going to stop busting my chops and believe me when I say everything is under control?"

"But, boss, the police are checking all your houses," said Jackson, leaning forward in his chair in the corner. "They're through more than half already. When they find where we've hidden Charlie and Tina, we're all going to be in a world of trouble."

"No problem! In a few days we'll move them to one of the other houses they've already checked."

"That will only get us so far, boss." Vi leaned nonchalantly against the wall. "As soon as they find the modifications we made to the house where we stashed them, they'll know we've moved them. They'll just start looking through the other houses again. We can't stay ahead of them much longer. I say we cut them loose and make a run for it."

"Oh you do, do you?" Crackers looked at Jackson and Grimsby. "Do you two agree with Vi here?"

They both nodded vigorously.

"Well, I have a score to settle with this Dusty character, and until I do no one is making a run for it!" he shouted. "Our prisoners stay right where they are until I say otherwise! Is that clear enough for the three of you?"

Grimsby, from his chair in front of the desk, gulped and nodded. Vi and Jackson nodded in unison as well.

"I'm glad to hear it," Crackers said sarcastically. "Now, I'm tired of looking at you. So get out of here. And I don't want to see any of you for a few days, is that clear?"

"Why?" Vi asked nervously. "What are you planning?"

"Just a little surprise for our good friend Dusty. Nothing to worry your little heads about. But I'll tell you this: Dusty took something from me and I'm going to take something from him."

"What are you going to take of his, boss?" Grimsby said. "Maybe we could help."

"Oh, you want to help, do you, Grimsby? Well, this time I won't need help. The less you know, the better."

"But boss—"

"That's enough! Now, all of you get out of here before I lose my temper!"

The three co-conspirators practically fled while Crackers sat there grinning.

As she was leaving, Vi turned back at the door and gave Crackers a concerned look. Then she turned and walked out, pulling the door closed behind her.

Crackers listened to their footsteps recede and smiled all the more broadly.

It's payback time, Dusty, he thought.

CHAPTER
FORTY-NINE

FIRST THING THE NEXT MORNING, Dusty got the cold pack from the freezer, wrapped it in the hand towel, and held it on his left knee for fifteen minutes. Afterward he headed off to breakfast. Though he still limped a bit, he found that it wasn't as pronounced. Indeed, he felt better.

Following breakfast, he managed to have a shower. Just as he was getting out, he heard the phone ring.

"Hello?" he answered, having hurried to the bedside from the bathroom.

"It's Cindy. How's your leg today?"

"Much better, thank you. Still not quite back to normal, but much better than yesterday. I managed to make it to breakfast and take a shower on my own. The cold pack really helped."

"That's great! Maybe what you need, in addition to the cold pack, is a nice leisurely walk. What do you say?"

"Are you inviting me to join you?" Dusty asked.

"Of course, silly."

"I'd be up for giving it a try. But we'll have to quit when my knee has had enough."

"Fair enough. How about I pick you up in half an hour?"

"Works for me. I'll meet you out front."

• • •

Thirty minutes later, Dusty was waiting just outside the front door of the hotel, leaning against the wall, when Cindy pulled up.

"Hop in," she said. "There are some nice walking trails over by the leisure center. Because of your knee, though, it would be better to drive there."

In minutes, Cindy pulled into a large parking lot shaded by large elm trees. They headed to a dirt trail that wound through the trees. Dusty took her hand as they strolled down the path. They walked a bit slower than normal due to the slight stiffness in Dusty's knee, but at the end of the walk the knee felt much looser.

They made plans to go to church together the next day, which would give them a chance to see Mrs. Wilcox again.

On the way home they found a luggage store where Dusty bought a small suitcase for his trip.

When Cindy dropped Dusty back at the hotel, she came around the car to give him a hug.

"See you tomorrow," she said. "I'll pick you up if you like."

"Sure. That would be great."

Dusty smiled as Cindy waved, got into her car, and drove off.

● ● ●

After church the next day, they found Mrs. Wilcox outside the front of the building, enjoying the bright sunshine.

"So no word on your missing friends yet?" Mrs. Wilcox asked when she spotted them.

"Not yet," Dusty said. "But I'm hoping the police find them soon."

Mrs. Wilcox turned to him. "Cindy says that you're leaving us."

"Just for a short time. Enough time to go back home and pay off a loan. Now that I have the money, the sooner I pay it the better."

She nodded. "I hope the both of you will come visit me when Dusty returns."

"Of course we will, Mrs. Wilcox. Won't we, Dusty?" Cindy turned to regard him.

"For sure! You can count on it, Mrs. Wilcox."

The older woman took Cindy and Dusty by the hand. "Now, I think it's time you two kids stopped calling me Mrs. Wilcox and called me by the name my friends use. I mean, it only seems right if you're going to come visit when you're back in town, don't you think? So please call me Ruth."

"It's a deal, Ruth," Cindy said. "And thanks."

Cindy and Dusty said goodbye to her and then returned to the hotel to have lunch together in the restaurant.

After eating, Cindy reached for her purse. She tucked a wayward strand of hair behind her ear.

"I'll see you again tomorrow around 8:00 p.m.," she said. "We should get to the train station at about 9:15… and according to the train schedule you can start boarding at 10:00 p.m. It departs at 11:00."

He looked longingly into her eyes. "How about we get there early… on the off-chance the train is early. We can have supper in Saskatoon."

"Okay, sure. Sounds like a plan." Cindy smiled. "See you at six o'clock."

Before standing to go, she gave him a hug and soft kiss on the cheek.

CHAPTER
FIFTY

IN THE MORNING, DUSTY'S KNEE felt very close to being back to normal. He had used the cold pack after his walk with Cindy. He now headed to breakfast with barely any sign of a limp.

While he was eating his favorite meal of eggs, bacon, and toast, Tom and Wendy came by his table.

"Are you all packed and ready?" Wendy asked.

"Just about. There are a few items left to take care of, but then all I have to do is wait for Cindy to pick me up. I really appreciate all your help with finances when I first arrived."

"It was our pleasure," Tom said. "Well, we'll leave you to finish your meal. If you need us for anything, you know where to find us."

The rest of the day passed uneventfully, and once Dusty had packed all his things in the new suitcase, he wandered towards the tiny bookstore in the hotel lobby. He chose a good action book to read on the train.

Before he knew it, it was six o'clock and he found himself pacing nervously around his hotel room, waiting for Cindy to show up.

At five minutes past six, there was a knock at the door.

Dusty rushed to the door and flung it open. But it wasn't Cindy standing there with a smile on her beautiful face. Instead it was Wendy, looking a bit distraught. She held a folded piece of paper to him.

Dusty took the paper and noticed his name scrawled across it in crude handwriting. After unfolding it, he read the note:

If you want to see Cindy alive again, meet me at the Saskatoon train station at nine o'clock. Come alone. And bring my money with you.

Crackers

All the blood drained from his face. His knees buckled, but Wendy caught him and helped him over to the bed to lie down. Then she went into the bathroom and ran a facecloth under cold water. She placed it on Dusty's forehead.

"Just lie here for a bit," she said. "I'll go get Tom and be right back."

As she left him, he heard the door open and a moment later softly click shut.

He closed his eyes and thought about the note. How on earth had Crackers gotten ahold of Cindy? If he hurt her in any way, Dusty didn't know what he'd do... but he was pretty sure Crackers wouldn't like it.

He ran though his memories of Cindy smiling and laughing, the touch of her hand on his and how he felt when he was around her...

He must have dozed off, because the next thing he knew Wendy was gently shaking him.

"Are you okay, Dusty? Tom's here and he says we can drive you to Saskatoon to get Cindy back. I've already arranged for someone to cover the front desk while we're gone."

Dusty blinked a few times, trying to absorb what Wendy was saying. Then he recalled that Crackers had snatched Cindy and sat bolt upright in bed.

"Easy, Dusty," Tom said. "Just lay back. You've had a big shock."

Dusty lowered himself onto the bed and looked up into the concerned faces of the owners of the hotel. He realized they had become good friends and were now a lifeline... a shoulder to lean on until he had Cindy safe and sound in his arms again.

That was, if he ever got her back at all.

"What time is it?" Dusty asked.

"6:45," Tom said.

"And how long does it take to drive to the train station in Saskatoon?"

"About an hour."

"Do you want us to call the police and let them know what happened to Cindy?" Tom asked.

Wendy looked at him closely. "The note said for Dusty to come alone. I told you that."

He nodded. "I know, but it might still be a good idea to let Inspector Baxter know."

"I can't chance it," Dusty murmured. "I could never forgive myself if anything happened to Cindy. Anyway, I'm going to rest some more. I didn't sleep too well last night. Kept thinking about going back to Edmonton and facing that loan shark again. The last time I faced him, it wasn't too pleasant. Plus, this news about Cindy has taken a toll on me. Will you wake me in about thirty minutes?"

"Sure, dear." Wendy patted his shoulder affectionately. "You just rest."

It seemed to Dusty that he had just closed his eyes when he heard another round of knocking. Groggily he sat up in bed, rubbed his eyes, and stumbled to the door.

Tom and Wendy were there.

"Thirty minutes is up," Tom said. "We should go soon in case traffic is bad in Saskatoon. For Cindy's sake, it's probably best that we aren't late."

Before leaving, they stopped at the front office to open the safe and get the duffel with the hundred grand in it. Once that was done, they went out the back of the hotel where Tom and Wendy's car was parked.

Throwing the suitcase and duffel in the trunk, Tom and Wendy got in the front and Dusty sat in the rear. They were off.

CHAPTER
FIFTY-ONE

THE DRIVE TO THE TRAIN station went a lot faster than Dusty expected, and before he knew it they had arrived. The time was 8:45, due to heavy traffic.

As soon as the car stopped, Dusty leaped out and dashed to the trunk. Tom popped it open and Dusty grabbed the duffel.

"Is that all you're taking with you?" Tom asked as all three of them hurried to the station's double doors.

"For now it is," Dusty said. "If I get Cindy back, I may still catch the train to Edmonton tonight. I'll need my suitcase if that happens. But for now let's just leave it in the trunk."

Once inside they all stopped.

"Where do you think he'll have Cindy?" Wendy asked.

"I'm not sure." Dusty looked around, and other than a ticket counter there wasn't much to see. He spied a few people sitting or lying down on the seats. There were about two dozen chairs arranged in long lines.

He didn't see Cindy or Crackers.

Dusty went back outside and took note of the train, sitting on the tracks a couple hundred yards away. He started that way with Tom and Wendy, but was soon stopped by a train station employee.

"Only passengers beyond this point, folks," the man said.

Dusty didn't have a ticket yet, so he decided to go back inside and buy one.

"I'm not sure what more you can do," he said to Tom and Wendy once he had the ticket in hand. "They won't let you on the train without a ticket. I suppose you could hang out here in the station... if I'm not back in twenty minutes, maybe find a security guard to come look for me. Or, if you want to head home, I understand. I'm sure everything will be okay."

"We're not leaving until we know you and Cindy are safe," Wendy insisted.

Tom nodded in agreement.

"Fair enough," Dusty said. "I'll see you in a bit then."

He headed towards the tracks while Tom and Wendy watched through the windows from inside the terminal.

When Dusty got back to the employee, the fellow took a look at his ticket and waved him through. The closer Dusty got to the train, the more his legs felt like lead, but he pushed himself on.

All the train's doors were open. He climbed the first set of steps and entered at the back of the train. He found himself in a hallway with closed doors on one side and windows on the other. He walked on.

Next he came to a set of doors and pushed through, leaving the first train car and stepping onto a platform between the cars. He pushed open the door to enter the next car.

This car was the same as the first, and so was the third and fourth car. He figured those were all filled with private compartments.

Coach seating came next, and it was set up much the same way as a bus, with two seats on either side of the aisle. This car was empty, but then again the train wasn't due to leave for another two hours.

He pushed on to the next car, and when he entered he saw just one person sitting in a seat in the middle.

When he got closer, he saw that it was Cindy.

"Cindy!" Dusty rushed forward and fell on his knees, setting his bag beside her seat. He saw that she was tied up and gagged, so he removed the gag.

"Oh, Dusty, I'm so glad you came!" she said. "I've been so scared."

"Hold still and I'll have you free in no time."

He started working on the knots that bound her. When he got her arms untied, she threw them around him and hugged him.

As he got to work untying her feet, the door to the car suddenly burst open ahead of him. In stepped Crackers, wearing a malicious grin on his face. The man's arms hung loosely by his side and in his right hand he held a gun.

"Get on your feet, you worthless piece of scum," Crackers hollered. "Or I'll shoot you right where you are. And then I'll shoot your girlfriend!"

Dusty slowly got to his feet, putting his hands up in surrender.

Crackers was about ten feet away, standing right in front of the door he had just come through. "Now, first things first: where is my money?"

"Uh, it's right here." Dusty pointed to the small duffel on the floor.

Crackers looked at the bag and scowled. "In that puny thing? How much did you bring?"

"One hundred thousand."

"One hundred thousand! You stole five million from me and all you have left is one hundred thousand? Did you think I'd be pleased by that? I'll show you how pleased I am!" Crackers turned slightly and aimed his gun at Cindy. "You took something important from me, and now I'm gonna take something important from you!"

But Dusty wasn't listening anymore. When Crackers turned the gun towards Cindy, fury rose up inside him. With his fists balled up, he charged at Crackers.

Startled, Crackers backed up and turned the gun towards Dusty. But just then the door behind him exploded open, throwing Crackers to the floor and sending him sprawling into the aisle. The gun was knocked loose and skittered a few feet past his outstretched hand.

Dusty skidded to a halt and gingerly picked up the gun. He then looked up to see who had opened the door. There, with a gun in one hand and a coffee in the other, stood none other than Inspector Baxter. He wore a big grin on his face.

Two officers slid past the inspector and hauled Crackers to his feet, handcuffing his hands behind his back.

"You have the right to remain silent…"

CHAPTER
FIFTY-TWO

DUSTY WAS A BIT CONFUSED in the morning when he woke up in his hotel room. Hadn't he gone to the train station in Saskatoon?

It all came back in a rush. He'd come back to Duggan with Cindy and she was safe. Crackers had been apprehended. Inspector Baxter had shown up shortly before the train's departure, and Tom and Wendy had sent him after Dusty.

With a stab of excitement, Dusty thought he'd finally get to see Charlie and Tina safe and sound. Surely Crackers would tell the police where they were, now that he was in custody—maybe in exchange for a slightly reduced sentence for kidnapping and attempted murder. It looked like the Grub would have to wait a bit longer for his money.

Dusty's stomach was in knots when he went for breakfast and he ended up hardly eating a bite. How many weeks had it been since his friends' disappearance? Or had it been months? He tried to recall when he had first arrived in Duggan. In some ways, it felt like just a few weeks ago. But in other ways, especially with Cindy, it felt like he'd been there for a couple of years.

After breakfast Dusty went back to his room and called Cindy, but there was no answer.

He hung up the phone just in time to hear a knock at his door. When he opened it, the smiling faces of Charlie, Tina, Cindy, Tom, Wendy, and Inspector Baxter were looking back at him. All of them laughed at the shocked expression on Dusty's face.

Charlie gave Dusty a hug. "You look surprised to see us."

"I was just thinking of you and hoping that I'd see you again now that Crackers was caught." Dusty pulled out of the hug and faced Baxter. "How did you end up at the train station last night? How did you know I'd be there?"

"We've been keeping a close eye on you, Dusty. So when you headed there yesterday one of the officers followed and I followed along behind. He told me you had gone to the train station."

"Smart, and how did you get Crackers to tell you where my friends were?"

"My boss gave me approval to waive the kidnapping charges if he gave up the information. Which he did. But he'll still be charged with bank robbery."

Tina leaned in for a hug as well. "It's good to see you, Dusty."

"It's good to see you both," he said. "But why didn't you call and let me know you were coming?"

"Simple," Tina told him. "We wanted to surprise you. And it looks like it worked."

Cindy, Tom, and Wendy stood back, smiling. Even Baxter sported a tiny smile to see the friends reunited.

"Now that we're finally free, when are we going to blow this place?" Charlie asked.

Tina elbowed him in the ribs. "Don't be rude, Charlie. Dusty has a girlfriend now."

Charlie rubbed his ribs. "Sorry, Dusty, I forgot." He turned to Cindy. "Sorry, I've been cooped up for so long that I've forgotten my manners."

Cindy smiled at Charlie. "That's okay. It's perfectly understandable. I'm on vacation right now, so why don't the four of us go to Edmonton together?"

"How are we going to get there?" Tina asked. "Take the train?"

Charlie jangled the car keys in his hand. "We'll pile into the car and head out."

"The car has been sitting for weeks," Dusty reminded them. "It may not even run."

"Nonsense." Charlie shook his head. "The car will be fine. How far away is it from here?"

"Not far. It's close to the warehouse where I've been working."

As they walked towards the front door of the hotel, Dusty sidled up close to Cindy. "How did you know my friends would be coming here?" he asked softly.

"I didn't. I just came over to surprise you and bumped into them on the way to your room."

"I'm glad you came." Dusty took her hand in his. "Do you still have that envelope you were to give to Red for me?"

"I do." She pulled the envelope out of her pocket.

Dusty took it from her. "Since you're coming with us to Edmonton, give me a minute to see if Wendy or Tom can give this to Red."

In the lobby, he pulled Tom and Wendy aside and brought them up to speed on what he needed.

"Of course," Wendy said, beaming. "We'll give this to him tomorrow. This is so exciting!"

Dusty rejoined his friends and Baxter led them back to the cruiser. They all squeezed themselves inside as the inspector drove them to the street where Charlie's car was still parked after all this time. Tom and Wendy followed in their car.

When they all arrived Charlie hopped out and unlocked the door to his car. He put the key in the ignition. The engine sputtered a bit before roaring to life.

"There," he said, lowering the window. He affectionately patted the side of the car. "I told you this baby would start up."

"Are you sure you need to leave right away?" Wendy asked. "We'll miss you."

Dusty turned to her, suddenly feeling emotional to leave his new friends behind, even though he knew he would see them again.

"I'll be back to Duggan before too long," he said, smiling.

Once the friends were all in the car, Cindy turned to Dusty as though only now coming to a realization.

"Shoot," she said. "I don't have anything packed for this trip. Can we swing by my place so I can throw a few things together?"

"Sure, no problem," Dusty said.

They all waved goodbye to Tom and Wendy and the Inspector, then they were off. Cindy gave Charlie directions to get to her place.

It didn't take long before she was bounding back to the car with a midsized gym bag in her hand. She squeezed into the rear seat and placed her bag between her feet.

"Time to hit the open road!" Charlie hollered.

CHAPTER
FIFTY-THREE

AN HOUR LATER, STILL IN Duggan, Inspector Baxter placed a call to the police superintendent in Regina.

"Baxter, what have you got for me today?" Superintendent Sanderson said once the call was patched through.

"Well, sir, the bank robbers have all been caught and are under lock and key."

"Very good. Congratulations, my boy. Well done."

"Thank you, sir."

"And what of that fellow's missing friends? Any headway there? Did the bank robber... what was his name? Crumbs?"

"Crackers, sir."

"Right. Did this Crackers give you their location in exchange for leniency with the kidnapping charge?"

"He swears he had nothing to do with grabbing them. It was, as he put it, his 'idiot partners in crime.'"

"Yes, well... he still stashed them in one of his houses."

"That he did, sir. And yes, he did give up their location. And we did find them. That's actually where we caught the other three bank robbers—at that house. They were on babysitting duty, I guess. We set the two friends free and reunited them with Dusty. They're en route to Edmonton as we speak."

"Back to Alberta. Home to two of my favorite national parks... Jasper and Banff." Sanderson sighed wistfully. "Now, Baxter, do you have any loose ends you have to tie up or shall I be expecting you back here posthaste?"

"I just have one loose end, sir. But it shouldn't take long. I'll be on the highway soon and should be back in the office by lunch."

"Don't rush, my boy. After lunch will be perfectly fine. I'll expect you then."

With that the superintendent disconnected.

Baxter hung up the phone and headed off, saying his goodbyes as he went.

CHAPTER
FIFTY-FOUR

SOON THE FRIENDS WERE CRUISING down the highway, with Duggan receding in the rearview mirror. As Dusty looked out the window, he spied a group of people cleaning trash in the ditches. One of the workers glanced up just in time for Dusty to recognize him. It was Jerry!

"Dusty!" Cindy said. "Did you see who that was?"

"Sure did."

She sighed. "You seem pretty calm about it. It was just a few days ago that you got all heated up about what he'd done."

"Guess my experience at church calmed me down. I chose to forgive him."

"Good for you, Dusty." Cindy placed her hand gently on his arm. "You know, my dad was told by the police that Jerry is related somehow to Crackers."

"Who is this this Jerry fellow?" Tina asked while tucking a strand of hair behind her ear.

"He was the manager where Dusty worked," Cindy explained, looking at Dusty. "I didn't understand why he treated you so badly, Dusty... at least not until I found out he was part of Crackers's extended family."

"I don't mean to change the subject," Tina said from her seat behind the driver. "But I'll need a restroom soon."

And two hours later, Tina needed a bathroom yet again.

"It's going to take us forever to get to Edmonton with all these stops," Charlie moaned from the driver's seat. "I already feel like I've been on the road all day and it's only been a couple hours."

Tina said nothing. Dusty thought she might be feeling a little embarrassed.

"Relax, Charlie, we're not in a race here," Dusty reminded him. "We'll get there soon enough."

"I'll drive," Cindy suggested.

Charlie smiled. "That would be great. I'm getting sleepy. Not used to all the fresh air after being cooped up for weeks. We'll switch at the next place with a bathroom."

Twenty minutes later, Charlie took an exit and stopped in front of a rest stop building. Tina hopped out and disappeared inside while the rest of them traipsed inside more leisurely.

Before too long they were all back in the car, this time with Cindy behind the wheel. For the next leg of the trip Cindy and Dusty told the others about how they had met and all the adventures they had been on.

"Crackers and his buddies tried to kill you, Dusty?" Charlie said.

Tina let out a whistle. "They failed miserably then."

Next, Charlie and Tina told of how they had been grabbed and what it had been like to be kept as prisoners for weeks on end.

"What was the worst of it?" Cindy asked, glancing in the rearview mirror from time to time so she could see Charlie and Tina.

"The worst part was knowing we could be killed any time, and just not knowing when or if that day was coming," Tina said. "That first place must have had good soundproofing, because we never heard a sound until our door flew open."

"The worst part for me was the look in the fat guy's eyes," Charlie added. "I think they called him Grimsby. He looked like he would have shot us without a moment's hesitation if the others hadn't been with him."

Tina took a deep breath. "The guy they called Crackers terrified me. He looked like he wanted to throttle us every time we saw him… I'm glad that's all over now." She suddenly laughed, lightening the heavy mood. "One step down from terrifying was having to put up with Charlie's snoring."

"At least my snoring was only at night," Charlie retorted. "You two should have smelled her socks… and her feet! All day long! The reek was incredible."

Tina punched him in the arm.

Dusty lounged sideways in the front so he could watch Cindy and keep an eye on his friends.

The questions and light banter continued until they entered Edmonton. They stopped for one last gas fill-up. Then Charlie took the wheel again and headed to Dusty's place.

"So where am I staying?" Cindy asked.

Dusty slapped his head. "I can't believe I forgot to arrange that. Tina, do you have room at your place?"

"Sorry, Cindy, but I told my brother he could stay there while I was gone. Knowing him, it's a pigsty. It'll take me days to get it cleaned up and ready for a guest who isn't family."

"How about you, Charlie?" Dusty asked.

"No offence, Cindy, but I wouldn't be comfortable having a beautiful woman staying with me."

Cindy sighed. "I completely understand, Charlie."

"So I guess she's staying at your place, Dusty," Tina said.

Cindy touched Dusty's arm. "I can see you're a little freaked out about me staying at your place, but it's okay. I can sleep on the sofa."

"Well then, looks like it's settled," Charlie said. "I'll drop you both at Dusty's place."

Dusty stared at his shoes. The last time he had been in Edmonton he would have happily had Cindy come over to his place. But ever since that first visit to church in Duggan, something in him had changed. He wanted to treat Cindy like a princess.

But he guessed that it would be okay for her to sleep on the couch…

Wait a minute, he thought, suddenly having a better idea. *That's not what you offer a princess.*

A short while later, they were parked in front of Dusty's apartment building, their bags sitting on the sidewalk. Cindy was giving Charlie and Tina hugs.

"It was so nice to meet you both," Cindy said.

Charlie grinned. "The feeling is mutual, believe me."

Suddenly, two black Mercedes careened around the corner. One pulled in front of Charlie's car, effectively blocking it while the other slid in behind Charlie's car, just touching the bumper as it came to a complete stop.

Four burly men got out, two from each car.

CHAPTER
FIFTY-FIVE

CINDY STEPPED BEHIND DUSTY AND put her hand into his. Charlie and Tina looked around wildly. Dusty had a resigned look on his face.

"We knew you'd come back eventually," said one of the men as he stepped onto the sidewalk. "We've been watching your place for weeks."

The man wore black pants, black dress shoes, and a blue button-up dress shirt which was a tad tight in the shoulders. The other three were similarly dressed.

"I'm Mack," the man said with a sneer. "You owe Mr. Grubinski some money—and either you pay now, or we make an example of you. By the way, Mr. Grubinski sends his greetings."

One of the other men smacked his fist into the palm of his hand and grinned maliciously. "So what'll it be?"

"I uh, have the money," Dusty said.

"And where is it?" Mack asked. The other three burly men remained silent but poised for action.

Dusty pointed to the small duffel with their bags.

Mack motioned one of his men to open it. That man stepped forward, knelt by the duffel, and zipped it open.

"Lots of cash in here, Mack."

"How much, Ollie?"

The man named Ollie riffled through a few bundles, then did a quick count. "About a hundred grand, I'd say."

"Check the other luggage," Mack said.

"I only owe Mr. Grubinski fifty thousand," Dusty said. "That's half of what's in the duffel. There is no money in the other luggage."

Mack smiled widely, but it looked more like a grimace. "We'll see about that. I saw a newspaper article with your ugly mug in it that says that you got a five hundred thousand dollar reward for finding stolen money and I aim to find it. Also, fifty grand was what you owed about three weeks ago. Interest piles up quickly."

Dusty fumed, wishing he could do something. But he didn't think he'd have much of a chance against four heavily muscled men.

Mack waved another man forward who along with Ollie started opening all the luggage and tossing the contents out.

"When the boys are done here, Mr. Grubinski would like me to break a few of your bones for running out when he was expecting payment three weeks ago," Mack said, clearly enjoying the prospect of what he was about to do. "As soon as the boys finish, we'll get started. But maybe in a place that's a bit more private."

The two goons finished looking through all the bags. "There's no more money here," one of them reported.

"I told you there was no more money!" Dusty said angrily.

Mack grabbed Dusty by the front of the shirt and twisted it tight around Dusty's throat. "Where's the money, you little punk?"

He was interrupted by a police siren and Dusty looked up to see a cruiser pulling up. The officer got out and walked up to the group.

Mack released Dusty and turned to face the officer.

"What's going on here?" the officer asked with a frown.

"These men are robbing us." Dusty said while rubbing his throat.

"That's not true," Mack protested. He pointed to Dusty. "This man here owes our boss money. We're just here to collect."

"By throwing their clothes all over the sidewalk?" the officer asked.

"We'll clean it up." Mack motioned all three of his guys to do that and they sprang into action. Then Mack leaned down and picked up the small duffel containing the money.

The officer watched with a bemused expression while all the belongings were put back into the luggage.

"Is that the money owed your boss?" he asked Mack, indicating the duffel.

"Yes, it is."

"Then I suggest you finish cleaning up this sidewalk immediately and take the money and go... before I have to impound it for evidence."

"Evidence for what?" Mack asked suspiciously.

"I'll think of something."

The three other men quickly finished their job and closed the last bag. Together with Mack, they then hurried to their cars.

The car in front of Charlie's turned sharply onto the street and took off in a cloud of exhaust. The car behind backed up and sped off after it, filling Dusty's nose with the smell of burning rubber.

The officer turned to the friends. "I'm Officer Baxter. Pleased to meet you all."

Dusty looked at him, puzzled.

"Inspector Baxter is my brother. He called to let me know you were headed here, and he gave my your address." He looked squarely at Dusty. "He said it was on a form you filled out at the police station in Duggan. Anyway, my brother sounded a bit concerned on the phone and asked me to look after you. Glad I came by when I did. I've been driving by periodically today." He pulled a card out of his jacket pocket and handed it to Dusty. "Here. If you ever need me, don't hesitate to call."

Dusty took the card. "Thanks, Officer Baxter. And thank the good inspector for us, will you?"

"Absolutely." Officer Baxter shook everyone's hand before walking back to his cruiser, getting in, and driving off.

"All right, folks," Charlie said. "That was a bit of excitement, to say the least. But now it's time for me to get home and sleep in a real bed for once. You coming, Tina?"

Once Charlie and Tina had driven off, Cindy turned to Dusty. "You look very relaxed. More relaxed than I thought you would after giving them a hundred grand. In fact, last time we chatted you seemed rather angry about this loan shark and his goons."

"Yeah, it's weird. I didn't feel anything but contentment and peace today."

"Maybe God removed all those negative feelings the first day we went to church."

"You know, I think that's it. I haven't felt them since."

"Perhaps we should go to church more often," Cindy said smiling.

"If you're with me, I think I'd like that."

Dusty hefted both his bags and Cindy's and headed towards the front entrance of his building.

"What floor are you on?" Cindy asked.

"The third."

"Then you'd better let me help with the luggage. You're carrying my bag as well."

"No, I've got it."

Dusty staggered through the unlocked front door of the building, unlocked the door to the stairs, and began climbing. The bags banged into his legs with each step, throwing him off-balance. But he persevered.

When he got to his apartment door, he fished the keys out of his pocket again. He walked in and dropped the bags on the floor once they were both through.

"Welcome to my humble abode," Dusty said. He then picked up Cindy's bag again and carried it to the bedroom, setting it on the bed. "The bathroom is here. Feel free to freshen up if you like."

"Thanks, Dusty, I'd like that. But why did you bring my bag into the bedroom?"

"Because that's where you're sleeping."

"And where are you going to sleep?"

"On the sofa."

"This is your place. You should take the bedroom."

He shook his head. "Oh no, you're the guest. I'll be fine on the couch, trust me. And I won't take no for an answer."

Cindy went towards the bathroom, turned, and took three steps closer to Dusty. She kissed him, then skipped into the bathroom to freshen up.

CHAPTER
FIFTY-SIX

THE FIRST THING THAT ASSAILED Dusty's senses when he awoke was the smell of coffee and sizzle of food frying. Then a certain smell hit him too: bacon.

He sat up on the couch.

"Breakfast will be ready in ten minutes, sleepyhead," Cindy said, peeking out from the kitchen.

Dusty groaned, got up, and padded off to the bathroom.

After enjoying their breakfast, they both leaned back in their chairs with a sigh of contentment.

"That was fantastic," Dusty said.

"It was just eggs and bacon."

"Speaking of that... where did you get bacon and eggs from? And coffee, too, for that matter. I didn't have any here."

"I snagged your keys and went to the corner store this morning. But we need to go out and get more so we can eat more than just breakfast."

They were interrupted by the ringing of the telephone. Dusty had forgotten to cancel his home phone before fleeing to Saskatchewan. But he was about to feel quite glad that he hadn't.

"Hello?"

"Dusty! This is Aunt Mae," said the familiar voice on the other end of the line. "I got a nice letter here from you, not to mention a cashier's check made out to you for several hundred thousand dollars. No note about the check. Care to explain?"

Dusty could tell his aunt was bursting with curiosity. "It's a reward for finding money from a bank heist."

"Now this I must hear!" Aunt Mae said.

"I'll come down to Calgary soon to pick up the check," he said. "And I'll fill you in on all the details. You probably won't believe half of it. Oh, and I'll be bringing my girlfriend so you can meet her."

Aunt Mae squealed into the phone. "I can't wait, my boy. A tale to tell… and a girlfriend! You better not make me wait too long!" She laughed. "Seriously, come soon."

"I will, Aunt Mae, I will."

As Dusty hung up the phone, he noticed Cindy sitting up straighter at the small kitchen table.

"You mailed the cashier's check to your aunt?" she said. "That was brilliant. Otherwise those big dudes would have found it and taken it too."

"I sure did, but I can't take the credit for the idea. It came to me the first time we went to church." Dusty grinned at her. "It kept the money out of the hands of the Grub's goons."

A little later, Dusty and Cindy went off to the grocery store. They bought enough food for lunch and supper, then lugged it all back up to Dusty's third-floor apartment. For lunch they made ham, cheese, and tomato sandwiches.

While they were eating, the phone rang again. Dusty grabbed it.

"Dusty, my man!"

"Red? How did you get my number?"

"Directory assistance. I got a special delivery today from Wendy. A little present from you. How can I ever thank you? Fifty thousand dollars! It far exceeded even my biggest hopes of what you'd give me! You're the best, man."

"It was my pleasure. A small thank you for always having my back."

"I'll always be thankful for this, Dusty." His friend paused for a moment. "Sorry to cut this short, but I have to run. You've got to come back and visit some time, buddy."

"I will. Count on it. Say, did you find a new forklift driver?" Dusty asked.

"We did buddy. All is well."

He hung up and noticed Cindy leaning forward eagerly. She looked at him expectantly, with a raised eyebrow.

"What was that all about?" she asked.

"Red thanking me for the money."

"Just how much did you give him?"

"Fifty thousand."

Cindy whistled. "What are you planning to do with the remainder?"

"I'm not sure yet. Want to help me spend it?"

"Seriously?" Cindy went quiet for a few moments, thinking it over and chewing at the same time. "Well," she said a bit shyly, "I have always wanted to go to college."

Dusty smiled at her. "Sounds great. We can talk more about this later, though. For now, do you feel like going for a walk?"

"Sure. Where to?"

"Just around the neighborhood."

They finished lunch, cleaned up after themselves, and headed out. Once they were out on the sidewalk, Dusty took Cindy's hand and they walked off hand in hand.